ELIZABETH CODY KIMMEL

spin the bottle

DIAL BOOKS FOR YOUNG READERS

DIAL BOOKS FOR YOUNG READERS
A division of Penguin Young Readers Group
Published by The Penguin Group
Penguin Group (USA) Inc., 375 Hudson Street,
New York, NY 10014, U.S.A.
Penguin Group (Canada), 90 Eglinton Avenue East, Suite 700,
Toronto, Ontario, Canada M4P 2Y3 (a division of Pearson Penguin Canada Inc.)
Penguin Books Ltd, 80 Strand, London WC2R 0RL, England
Penguin Ireland, 25 St. Stephen's Green,
Dublin 2, Ireland (a division of Penguin Books Ltd)
Penguin Group (Australia), 250 Camberwell Road, Camberwell,
Victoria 3124, Australia (a division of Pearson Australia Group Pty Ltd)
Penguin Books India Pvt Ltd, 11 Community Centre,
Panchsheel Park, New Delhi - 110 017, India
Penguin Group (NZ), 67 Apollo Drive, Rosedale, North Shore 0632, New Zealand
(a division of Pearson New Zealand Ltd)
Penguin Books (South Africa) (Pty) Ltd, 24 Sturdee Avenue,
Rosebank, Johannesburg 2196, South Africa
Penguin Books Ltd, Registered Offices: 80 Strand,
London WC2R 0RL, England

The publisher does not have any control over and does not assume any
responsibility for author or third-party websites or their content.
Book design by Jasmin Rubero
Text set in Goudy Old Style
Printed in the U.S.A.

1 3 5 7 9 10 8 6 4 2

Kimmel, Elizabeth Cody
Spin the bottle / by Elizabeth Cody Kimmel
p.   cm.
Summary: When aspiring actress Phoebe and her best friend, the brainy Harper,
enter middle school, their friendship is briefly tested by Phoebe's admiration of
some of the drama club students and the intensity of her first crush,
but ultimately they find that their relationship can withstand
the stresses of their expanding lives.
ISBN: 978-0-8037-3191-2
[1. Middle schools—Fiction. 2. Schools—Fiction. 3. Best friends—Fiction.
4. Interpersonal relations—Fiction. Friendship—Fiction.] I. Title.
PZ7.K56475 Sp 2008
[Fic]—dc22   2007017127

For Ashton Crosby—in the classroom
and in the theater, always *sine qua non*

TABLE OF CONTENTS

· · · · · · · · · · · · · · · · · · ·

spin the bottle

CHAPTER ONE

The Stage Is Set

"Your mouth is hanging open a tiny bit," Harper whispered as we walked into the gymnasium where Activities Sign-Up was being held. Harper was my best friend, so she could say things like that and actually mean them in a nice way. And a person certainly didn't want their mouth hanging open on their very first day of middle school. A person most definitely didn't want their mouth hanging open when, after years of waiting, they were finally about to sign up for Drama Club.

Drama Club was the only thing about starting middle school I was truly happy about. Okay, we supposedly put on "plays" in elementary school, but they usually involved doing the chicken dance or getting costumed as one of the food groups. One time, seven of us had to be the Dancing Days of the Week. I was Waltzing Wednesday. Talent was not a requirement, and all performances took place in the gym. It was a nightmare. Singing tomatoes and dancing chickens had been known to throw up mid-song.

Since Harper had not yet decided what her passion was (she was currently toying with astronomy, art, medieval history, and quantum physics) and because we always liked to do things together, she was planning to join the Drama Club too. It was worth a little extra credit on the report card, and I had convinced Harper they might let her draw the program design for the productions. I mean, they'd be crazy not to let her try. Harper drew better than anybody I knew.

We stood with the other seventh graders like a group of confused cattle as a sour-looking woman with cropped white hair named Mrs. Harley made unnecessary announcements about the proper procedure for signing up for the various clubs.

Harper stood up very straight because she is a nice person and likes to be cooperative with authority figures.

"Boys and girls," Mrs. Harley called, narrowing her eyes.

Boys and girls? I felt like being called boys and

girls was one of the things we were supposed to leave behind in elementary school.

"QUIET!" barked Harper. She did it so fast, without changing her face in any way, that no one seemed to know where it had come from. But our group started to fall quiet. That's my Harper. She can do things like that because no one expects it from her. She's a Brain, and Brain's don't usually yell orders. Especially not on the first day of middle school.

"All right then," the woman said. "Listen carefully."

Mrs. Harley had a little lisp. She narrowed her eyes again and pursed her lips, like she already suspected a few of us of being criminals.

"Please visit each and every one of the activity tables before deciding what you want to sign up for. When you join a club, it is a commitment. Some clubs require more of your time than others. Use your heads, boys and girls. Do. Not. Overextend."

Mrs. Harley proceeded to repeat the same speech using slightly different words. When she finally commanded us to go forth and examine the activities tables, Harper hung back, letting the crowd surge forward first. I followed her lead.

For about the tenth time that day, I silently thanked my lucky stars that I had Harper with me. We'd been best friends since the second grade, and by this time she was almost like an extension of my own personality. When I found something insanely funny, Harper always did too. When Harper took an instant dislike to a person, it always turned out later that I had thought exactly the same thing. Every once in a while, we even found out we'd dreamt the same thing during the night.

"You're definitely, definitely joining Drama Club, right?" I said to Harper as we slowly walked into the center of the gym.

"You know I am, Pheebs," Harper replied, giving my arm a squeeze. I gazed at her, relieved. Harper's skin was lightly olive-colored, which meant even in the hideous fluorescent gymnasium light she looked pretty.

"And if they ever start a Physics Club, you'll join that with me, right?" Harper added.

"As long as you do all of the math and atom-splitting experiments, Harp, I'd be thrilled to join Physics Club with you."

Harper laughed, probably because she suspected I didn't know what an atom splitter really was, which was true, but I did know it had something to do with physics and sounded fairly comic.

"It is so strange to be here," I said. "Everything looks . . ."

"Wrong," Harper agreed. "Like it's not the real thing. Like . . ."

"Like it's a set for a play!" I said. "And when we all go home they'll take it away."

Harper nodded, smiling.

"Even the kids look weird," I added.

The boys I had known in the sixth grade, almost without exception, seemed to have mutated over the summer. Some of them looked like they'd been stretched out on a rack. I heard a few voices that had developed uncomfortable croaks and rasps. And many of the boys had grown their hair out so it fell over their eyes and noses and made them look like menacing Muppets. Some of the girls had transformed too. I noticed some sporting high heels and clutching purses, and bearing the outlines of discreet but obvious undergarments.

Other than going up half a shoe size during summer break, I was identical to the sixth-grade version of myself. My smooth places were still smooth. My flat places were still flat. I was essentially flawed and unremarkable, and I was used to it. Fortunately, Harper hadn't changed either. We'd been glued together for more than five years, and now we were remaining undeveloped together. It was comforting, in this Sea of Middle School Weirdness.

"Do you see Drama Club?" I asked anxiously.

Tables and displays for clubs lined each wall. Some of the clubs, like the one called "School Yearbook

Committee," had crowds of people around. Others, like "Latin Club," had attracted no one. That table was deserted except for one lone Latin Club representative, who was sadly fiddling with a Game Boy.

"Over there," Harper said, pointing.

Yes. There it was. The Monroe Middle School Drama Club banner hung proudly over a large table covered with old posters and programs from productions of yesteryear. I knew them all, because I'd faithfully attended every production for two years. I'd seen such classics as *Once Upon a Mattress, Annie, Bye Bye Birdie,* and *A Christmas Carol,* all of which were reviewed in the local newspaper with photos and everything. I knew the name of every person who'd had a lead part in these shows from studying the programs, and that's how I knew that the girl sitting behind the Drama Club table was the legendary Delilah Fortescue.

In the world of middle school theater, Delilah was an intergalactic celebrity. She and Bud Gelcho were now ninth graders, and they'd both gotten starring roles for the last three shows running. I'd heard Bud and Delilah had even started dating over the summer.

"Oh geez, Harper, do you see who's sitting there?" I whispered urgently.

Harper shook her head. She'd come to many of

the Drama Club shows with me, but she didn't have quite the encyclopedic knowledge of names, faces, and theatrical resumes that I did. Go figure.

"It's Delilah Fortescue," I whispered reverently.

"Come on, a space just opened up," Harper said. "Let's scoot over there while there's no line."

This was the great thing about Harper. When I was with her, I felt more solid, more sure. Our brain patterns were in perfect sync. But when I was alone, it was like the Inner Me and the Outer Me split. The Inner Me was unique, edgy, artistic, and possibly mesmerizing. That's who I was around Harper. But sometimes if I was by myself, the Inner Me got wrapped up like a mummy by the Outer Me. I was suddenly clumsy, nervous, and said mortifyingly stupid things. The only time this didn't seem to apply was if I was acting. My Waltzing Wednesday, for example, was not clumsy or nervous. She was the picture of poise and grace.

Harper now took my arm and pulled me toward the Drama Club table. Thank heaven. This was not the time I wanted the Outer Me to take control and say and do a bunch of supremely idiotic things.

Suddenly I felt like I'd been shot through an atom splitter. I seemed to have beamed through time and space, because I was now standing right in front of Delilah Fortescue, who was giving me a wide smile.

To this day, I swear I don't remember actually walking across that room.

"Hi there! I'm Delilah. Are you guys interested in signing up for Drama Club?" I'd never seen Delilah Fortescue close up. It was hard to see her whole face because she was wearing a ball cap that said "Lion King," and it was pulled down low over her eyes. I wanted to yank it off so I could get a good look at her.

"I'm Harper," Harper said. I loved that Harper never minded talking first. Now that she had broken the ice, I was ready to forge ahead. I took a deep breath.

"I'm Phoebe," I said. "We'd both like to sign up for Drama Club."

"Great!" Delilah exclaimed, and I wondered if their numbers were low so far this year, because she sounded so happy that we were joining. "Do you guys both act?"

"I do," I said. I felt like I was having an out-of-body experience. Part of me was standing there with Harper, cool as you please, chatting with Delilah Fortescue live and in the flesh. The other part of me was floating somewhere up by the basketball hoops, watching me chatting with Delilah and totally freaking out. Though she was kind of disguised by the hat, she was definitely the Delilah Fortescue I'd seen on stage, except her features seemed smaller and sort of plainer. She did have nice hair poking out from below the baseball cap—wavy and layered, almost honey-colored.

"Harper wants to do behind-the-scenes stuff. She could help design the programs. I mean, if you need someone. Because she can draw really well."

"Are you serious?" Delilah asked. "That is *awesome!* We always have a terrible time finding someone to handle the program design."

I beamed at Harper. This was actually going to work out.

"So what you'll need to do is just put your names and phone numbers on this list. There's a permission slip for parents to sign, because it's an after-school club and sometimes parents will need to pick you up because you miss the bus. Our orientation meeting is tomorrow at three thirty, and that's when Mr. Romeo, our drama teacher, will start auditions for the fall show. I don't know if you've already heard, but we're doing *Guys and Dolls*. If you don't know the show, trust me, it's going to be a blast!"

I vaguely knew the show—it was an oldie, and a musical. At this point, I didn't care if we were doing Handel's *Messiah* in faux velvet robes and Rollerblades. I just wanted to do something.

"But don't we need to study for auditions?" I asked.

Delilah laughed loudly and shook her head. I felt a flash of hot stupidity.

"No, it doesn't really work that way. I mean, if you know the show, that's all the better, but really all you have to do is pick a part and read the lines they give you. If you're auditioning for a singing part, you don't have to sing something from the show. It can be anything the pianist can figure out, which is just about everything. Seriously, it's no big deal. There will be handouts at the meeting with all the info. But to be honest, it's usually better to basically wing it. If you start putting too much thought into the, like, seven audition lines they give you, you'll over-act. You know?"

I nodded seriously. My feeling of stupidity was melting into gratitude. Delilah was right. It was better to read something fresh than to spend hours ana-lyzing it.

"Okay then, where do we sign?" I asked.

Delilah beamed as she held out the Drama Club clipboard.

Harper signed first, then handed the clipboard to me. I took two permission slips, one for each of us, and handed the clipboard back to Delilah.

"Okay, great! Congratulations, you guys, and wel-come to the Drama Club! Like I said, we're going to have a blast. We have work parties to get the set built, and pizza when rehearsal runs long. The whole group is so much fun to be around. You should try for an assistant producing job, Harper, so you can be at rehearsals too," Delilah said.

I turned to Harper and nodded earnestly. Harper *had* to be at rehearsals—it would be so much better than being there without her.

"Sometimes Mr. Romeo lets us play our own music on the sound system when we're warming up—it's like being at a stadium concert! Seriously, it's all great," Delilah said. Then she leaned forward and lowered her voice, adding, "Though my personal favorite is the traditional opening night game of Spin the Bottle."

Delilah gave both of us a conspiratorial grin, and I'm sorry to say that I just stood there like a fire hydrant. Just stood there, existing, saying nothing. The truth is I wasn't exactly sure I'd heard Delilah right. It sounded like she had said "Spin the Bottle." Could that be right? Even with Harper right next to me, the Outer Me moved rapidly into mummification mode and paralyzed my mouth. I glanced over at my best friend, who peered back at me, raising one eyebrow. One of us was going to have to speak.

"Huh?" I asked.

Brilliant.

Delilah put her hand over her mouth to cover her smile.

"I'm sorry. I'm totally not supposed to mention Spin the Bottle when you're just signing up! It's just you guys seem so cool, and the game is our big Drama Club secret. It's like, you know, a rite of initiation! It's totally, totally fun. I'm not trying to freak you out, honest."

"I'm not freaked out," Harper said, and I believed her. Harper was completely and thoroughly uninterested in boys, so I wasn't surprised that the idea of playing Spin the Bottle didn't make her stomach churn. I cannot say the same for myself.

I tried to look casual. You know, all, "Oh yeah, man, totally!" But my face wasn't cooperating.

"Forget I said anything," Delilah said, reaching over and squeezing my wrist. "Remember, auditions tomorrow at three thirty. Then the fun begins!"

I could sense there was another person in back of me, waiting for Delilah's attention.

"Okay, thanks," I said, and Harper and I stepped away from the table. I noticed a girl with blond curly hair and apple red cheeks standing right behind us, bouncing eagerly on her heels. "We'll see you then."

I wanted to immediately drag Harper into the corner to analyze Delilah and every word she had uttered, but Harper had spotted an "Artists' Collective" table, and wanted to go investigate it.

So I went along with her. I'd done what I'd come to do. I was officially a member of the Monroe Middle School Drama Club.

Though I'd apparently signed up for a bit more than I'd bargained for.

CHAPTER TWO

Close Encounter

Harper and I took the opportunity at recess to explore the far reaches of the playground. We had a private little recess nook in elementary school where we hung out and worked on our comic strip.

Harper and I had been writing and illustrating stories together since second grade. That might have been when we first discovered we had almost the exact same brain patterns. I'd draw a scene, and then Harper would take the pencil and continue it. Almost always, the picture she drew continued the story precisely the way I would have if I'd been drawing alone. When we finished our first comic book, you couldn't tell which work was Harper's and which was mine. Our handwriting was identical. Our people and animals were identical. We even drew little houses and suns and birds the same way. Harper could actually do real art too. Like, watercolor stuff. Which was way beyond me. But comics I could do. It was our thing.

I was looking forward to getting back to work on the strip. Hopefully we'd find a suitable hideaway, a place we could work or talk without other people coming over and wanting to see what we were doing. After a brief exploration, we found some old swings set apart from the playing fields. Nobody else seemed interested in them, so Harper and I had the set to ourselves.

"I'm nervous," I said to Harper. We were crouched side by side on a log behind the swings, with our current comic strip, "My Not So Alien Life," in a notebook spread over both our laps.

"Nervous about what in particular?" she asked. She leaned over the notebook as she doodled a little spaceman with spastic rays coming out of his head.

"Well, for starters, everything. Do you think they're going to be really strict this year? Because Mrs. Teeky let a lot slide in sixth grade. Practically no one ever got in trouble, except Anthony Swister, who is basically a criminal anyway. And I hear the homework load is really serious in seventh grade. What if I can't keep up with the work? Mrs. Teeky never gave more than one math sheet and optional reading pages." I sighed. The scholastic world was one of the few places Harper's brain waves did not overlap with mine. "Straight A's come easy to you, Harp, but what if I was just coasting by? And what about the food?! That girl from gym last year, the one with dreadlocks whose name nobody ever really knew, she said her sister heard an eighth grader actually found a Band-Aid in his—"

"Pheebs, okay. Stop," Harper said, tucking a lock of straight, chocolate-colored hair behind one tiny ear. "First of all, the Band-Aid in the chicken chow mein is an urban legend. Apocryphal."

"I don't know what that means," I said.

"A made-up story everyone latches on to as truth. The Band-Aid in the chicken chow mein story gets told at every school, every year."

"I actually heard it was in the spaghetti with marinara sauce."

"The details always shift slightly," Harper assured me. "As for discipline, our homeroom teacher didn't exactly come off like a prison guard. I like him."

Harper and I both had Mr. Wick, which was a huge blessing, and I had to agree that he seemed like a pretty decent guy. He kept his own Burmese python in an aquarium in the classroom, which was cool. He was sort of cute too, and that didn't hurt. I took the pen out of Harper's hand and began to draw a little space dog next to her space guy. After some thought, I gave the dog his own set of spastic rays.

"And I don't think we need to worry about the work," Harper continued, as she leaned against me to watch me draw. "Sixth-grade work is designed for sixth graders. Mrs. Teeky's class would be boring to us now. We've, you know . . . evolved. Into seventh graders. And we have each other. I can help you with math and science, and you can help me with social studies. We have nothing to worry about, I promise."

It *would* be good to have her helping on some of the math and science, I thought, though to be honest, Harper didn't need any assistance with social studies. Harper was a Brain, but not a regular one—she downplayed it and everything, but really, Harper's IQ ought to be declared a national treasure.

"Well, then there's the Drama Club audition tomorrow," I said. Just saying it out loud made my stomach lurch.

"Yeah," Harper said. "I can understand how you'd be nervous about that. I could never do it, that's for sure. But Pheebs, this is *you* we're talking about. You did two summer sessions at Young Protégé Acting Camp. You have a subscription to *American Theater Magazine*. You can morph into anybody, and I ought to know. I'd give anything to be able to get up in front of people like that. It's amazing what you can do. I really don't think you have to worry about a seven-line audition."

Though Harper probably had more information stored in her brain than any seventh grader in the country, I knew she didn't know that much about plays or auditions. Still, her reassurance made me feel better. Just sitting next to her had a tranquilizing effect. In all the strangeness of middle school, Harper was exactly as she'd always been. Her mocha brown hair was long and completely straight and always had a great shine to it. Her eyes were dark and almond shaped. She was neither tall nor short, neither hefty nor scrawny. She wore sensible, un-trendy clothes like jeans and double layered T-shirts. And she always smelled like peppermint.

There was something else too, that I couldn't put my finger on. Something Harper had. Crazy stuff could be going on all around her, but she always stayed calm. "Centered," as my mom would say. Elementary school had never ruffled her, and it didn't look like middle school would either. Not that Harper wasn't a worrier. She could be a world-class worrier. But she worried about things like global warming, and the ozone layer. She obsessed over genetically engineered food sources and super-viruses. Harper didn't waste any of her incredible brain fussing about her school life. At least, she hadn't in the time I'd known her.

"Google the play tonight, and find a rundown of the parts. Then at least you'll know who you want to audition for when you get there tomorrow."

"Should I even go for a big part?" I asked. "That's like eighth- and ninth-grader stuff, probably."

"Maybe," Harper said. She began to sketch a little alien version of Mrs. Harley, whose squinty eyes were now shooting laser beams. "But there's no point in auditioning for a tiny part. You're you. You'll stand out. Read for a big one, and leave the rest up to Mr. Romeo. If that's his real name."

"Why wouldn't it be his real name?" I asked.

"How many Romeos do you know?" Harper asked. It was true. I'd never known anyone with the name Romeo, except for our neighbor's pug puppy.

"You have a point," I said. "Maybe it's a stage name."

"Maybe he should rethink it," Harper said. "Anyway, I hope he's nicer than Mrs. Harley. She's a piece of work. Imagine having *her* for homeroom."

I narrowed my eyes and pursed my lips in Mrs. Harley's trademark fashion.

"Boyth and girlth," I droned. Then I breathed deeply through my nose the way Mrs. Harley did, keeping my lips pursed and my chin tilted up.

"Boyths and girlths, it ith very important you under-thand that a bug crawled up my—"

Harper swatted me on the arm, giggling insanely. "That's her! That's exactly her!"

"Thettle down, thudenth," I said, making my eyes into little slits and staring down my nose at Harper.

Harper flapped her hands at me like she was try-ing to fan me away. She was so incapacitated by silent laughter, I was worried she might accidentally pee.

"Pheebs," Harper finally wheezed. "You gotta stop. I can't take it."

"It's only acting, dahling," I drawled. I produced a roll of peppermint Mentos chewy mints from my jacket pocket. I'd been saving them for later, but now I offered Harper the roll.

"Mentos!" Harper exclaimed, helping herself to two.

"Don't drink Pepsi right after you eat them," I cau-tioned. "A girl did that, and her stomach blew up."

"Another urban legend," Harper said, popping both mints into her mouth at the same time.

"Acropiphal," I said.

Harper laughed. "*Apocryphal*. Now," she com-manded, her cheeks bulging out like a chipmunk's, "let's swing."

We were still the only people by the old swing set. I didn't mind occasionally mingling with the other girls, but Harper called most of them Tiny Minds and didn't like to be around them. Harper could be kind of . . . stuck-up about other people sometimes. But she never acted superior to me. And there really wasn't anyone else I wanted to hang out with anyway. Harper hopped into a swing and twisted the chains above her head, then let go and spun around in circles, her hair flying out in a perfect arc. She extended both toes in ballerina points as she perched on the swing.

"I wish I could be more like you," I suddenly said, pausing at the swing next to hers. "You don't seem the tiniest bit freaked by middle school. You don't ever worry about what people think about you."

"That's because I don't *care* what people think about me," Harper said, pumping her pointed toes to start swinging. "You know that. And you also know there are plenty of things I'm not calm about. The deforestation of the Amazon, for one. Arctic drilling for another. Avian flu. Global warming. *Those* are things that rattle me. What Tiny Minds have to say about my clothes or my face or my personality is meaningless. They're not my people. *You're* my people."

I sighed and sat down on my swing.

"You're my people too, Harper. But I still worry, you know, how I come across."

Harper, who'd been swinging fairly high, abruptly let go of the swing, soared through the air, and landed solidly, both feet planted firmly on the woodchips.

"Pheebs, you come across exactly how you are, which is a very funny and generous person, and an amazing actress and comic strip writer. A deep thinker too. And you make me laugh—you make me have fun even when I think I can't."

I flashed the Mrs. Harley face again.

Harper giggled. "If it wasn't for you," she said, "I'd be like Eeyore all the time, worrying about the planet."

"Yeah but—"

"You are *truly authentic,*" Harper said with serious conviction. "Why do you think you're my best friend?" She paused. "But you are, and I mean this in the nicest possible way, a little obsessive about what the rest of the world thinks of you, and compulsive in the behavior patterns that promulgate it."

"Okay," I said, because I wasn't sure exactly what that meant but sensed it was more than likely true.

"And I think the reason you're feeling it right now is because this audition tomorrow is a symbol," Harper continued.

"A symbol for what?" I asked. Harper got back on the swing next to me. We started to swing in tandem, matching each other's speed exactly.

"A symbol of judgment. Because beyond just worrying about what other people think of you, at this audition you're essentially *asking* to be judged. You're getting up there and implicitly giving everyone permission to formulate an opinion about you."

Usually I thought it was cool when Harper used big words. But today it was making me more nervous.

"I know you're trying to help me, Harp, but frankly I'm starting to feel sick," I said, clutching my stomach with one hand.

"Stop swinging," Harper said quickly. "And have one of your Mentos. Peppermint is really calming to the stomach. And you know, forget about what I said. You're going to kick butt and take names at this audition."

She sailed off the swing again, executing another perfect landing. I was afraid I'd land on my face, so I just stopped pumping and let the swing gradually come to a stop. Once my feet were on the ground, I did feel better.

"Harper, to tell you the truth, I'm starting to think this whole audition thing might not be such a good—"

Before I could finish my sentence and begin questioning my entire future, something whizzed past us, bounced off the old swing set with a ding, and shot into the bushes.

"What was that?" Harper asked, looking around.

If Harper didn't know what something was, believe me, nobody did. I was staring at the place in the bushes where the thing had disappeared. And that's when it happened.

He came out of nowhere, walking toward me and Harper. And if you'd asked me later, I would have sworn that there were fireworks blasting overhead and a shooting star arcing through the sky. My stomach plunged into my shoes.

He was like no other boy I'd ever seen. He had jet-black hair and wide dark eyes. He was long and lanky and lean, wearing a faded Greenpeace T-shirt and worn jeans. He looked like a rock star and walked like royalty.

He stopped when he saw Harper and me. I sat frozen on the swing. His mouth opened. He was definitely going to say something. He turned to me. The entire universe seemed to drop away.

"Anyone seen a Frisbee?"

CHAPTER THREE

Performance Anxiety

I forgot I'd been momentarily considering not trying out for the play, because I'd been plunged into a walking coma by the encounter with this boy. With this Object of My Affection. With this . . . OOMA.

Although he'd found his Frisbee in seconds, and smiled and walked away, I managed to find hundreds of little details to play over in my mind. I can't explain it. It was the way he looked, yeah. And the way he walked, and his hair and his jeans. But there was also something else. A big YES ringing through the universe. Something that shouted THAT ONE.

Was this one of those things they don't tell you about middle school? Did this happen to other seventh-grade girls? Was it normal? And most importantly, *what was I supposed to do now?*

I had an obsessive, heart-pounding conversation with Harper that night about the OOMA. Except that all the obsessing and heart pounding was one-sided. Harper thought the guy seemed nice, but she didn't share my belief that he was the center of the biophysical universe. She patiently listened while I blabbered on about him, but she didn't have much to offer in the way of advice. And I needed advice.

"The thing is, and I know I've said this already, I'm just totally stumped on what I'm supposed to do," I said to Harper earnestly.

"Right," Harper responded.

You see, what I needed at this moment was one of Harper's important talks, full of long words and psychological thingies and biological behaviorial whadyacallits. But for once, all she had was a one-word answer. Usually our evening phone conversations involved a lot of me doing my imitations of people and things that had happened that day. Harper always begged for specific requests—do the gym teacher when the ball got stuck in the ceiling fan, do Melissa Spivak when she realized the trail of toilet paper was stuck to her, do Mr. Wick when the Burmese python tried to make a break for it. I knew this was probably what Harper wanted me to do now. But I had a different agenda.

"For example, do we, like, know each other now? You know, so that when I see him I'm all like 'Hey, yeah, glad you found that Frisbee'? Or would that seem too weird, that I'd remembered the Frisbee, like I'd been thinking about it or something. Is it better to pretend I don't really remember the specifics of our meeting? Or better to stress to him that I do? Would that make him feel special, or think that I'm stalking him?"

When it was clear that I had, for the moment, stopped asking questions, Harper said, "Dunno."

Dunno. From the girl of seven-syllable terms, she produced one that wasn't even a real word.

I tried not to be irritated. I mean, it didn't come as any great surprise that of all the hundreds of things Harper was an expert on, boys were not one of them. The only boy Harper had ever been profoundly affected by was Albert Einstein, and he was, you know. Old. Dead, actually. But Harper and I always shared our little life-quakes, and sorted them out together like they were science reports. Apparently, though, I was going to have to come up with the next move myself. I didn't know whether to draw hearts all over my notebook, keel over, or convince my parents to move to a different state.

The second day of middle school was slightly less strange than the first, and it passed pretty quickly. Before I knew it, it was almost 3:30, and Harper and I were headed for Drama Club. Now that the audition was looming, I had developed a full-blown case of nerves. This had never happened at Young Protégé Acting Camp. But in minutes, I was going to be rubbing elbows with older kids I had watched perform on this very stage. And auditioning in front of them. Everyone was going to see me. The thought of it pushed the OOMA right out of my brain.

I clutched Harper's arm.

"You're going to be fine," she said. "Phoebe. You. Are. Going. To. Be. Fine."

I managed to nod and shake my head at the same time.

"They're all here, Harp," I said, gesturing around the auditorium at all the people. "That big funny-looking guy? Ben Pfeiffer. He's like, hysterically funny. And that girl with the blue hat? Miranda Goetz, the one who sings so beautifully, people actually cry. That skinny guy dressed in black? Remember him?"

Harper shook her head.

"He's Chris Seligman. He's phenomenal—all dark and brooding. He usually plays bad guys. I mean, all of these people are amazing! In that second row down there I see Fedora Kravitz and Kelvin Black and Annabelle Peterson."

"There's that tall girl with the weird name," Harper said, pointing. "I remember her."

"Romalla Lee Um," I said. It truly *was* a weird name.

There were familiar faces everywhere I looked, people calling out to each other and yelling anecdotes about plays of yesteryear. The only one who seemed to be missing was the darkly glamorous Mia Kezdekian. She'd been absolutely amazing in *Annie*, and I was looking forward to seeing her live and in the flesh. Everyone else I'd come to see time and time again on this stage was right here. The Drama Club elite. Eek. What made me think I belonged here?

"This is like Piccadilly Circus," Harper said cryptically. "Grab one of those."

"Grab one of what?" I asked. Harper was pointing at a table next to the door that had a sign reading "*Guys and Dolls* Audition Pages" and stacks of photocopied pages. In my anxiety, I hadn't even noticed it. I grabbed the pages and followed Harper, who as usual had taken seats a few rows behind everyone else, out of the crowd. I sat down next to her, relieved to be able to safely watch everything going on, though at the same time wishing I were in the midst of it. I was in awe of these people but I also wanted to be one of them, which I wasn't, sitting two rows back with Harper.

"We will, we will—ROCK YOU!" boomed a loud male voice.

It was Ben Pfeiffer, dancing around on the front of the stage, his style half hip-hop, half spaz boy. He was soon joined by Bud Gelcho, who gave a loud war whoop. Ben greeted him with a shouted "Dude!" and they leaped toward each other and smacked stomachs. Fedora Kravitz and Romalla Lee Um had gone to huddle by the fire exit, where they were talking intently. Fedora interrupted their conversation momentarily to shout across the seats to Annabelle Peterson, who was wearing a leotard and leg warmers and was busy warming up and stretching as if she were planning to audition for *Swan Lake*.

"Annabelle, stop showing off and get over here! Romalla saw You Know Who at the place by the thing!"

"Maaaaaaaay meeeeeee maaaaaaah moooooooow mooooooooooooo . . . "

That was Miranda Goetz, walking down the center aisle right past where Harper and I were sitting, singing her scales and somehow making them sound like a work of art. Then I caught sight of the infamous Mia Kezdekian strolling casually in from the back door, resplendent in faded low-rise jeans and a T-shirt proclaiming "Women for Peace." Her beautiful face was unreadable, her long black hair flawless. How could someone look like that without a full-time team of stylists?

"That is gross!" came a high-pitched voice I didn't recognize.

"That is gross!" screamed Ben Pfeiffer, imitating the sound almost perfectly.

Chris Seligman, dressed in his signature black, paced a side aisle alone, warming up by chanting, "He beats his fists against the posts and still insists he sees the ghosts."

I glanced at Harper to see how she was reacting to this tantalizing view of actors and actresses in their natural habitat, but she had pulled out her math book and was starting her homework. Harper didn't really like being in groups of people. I totally sympathized. But my attention was drawn back to the front of the room by Kelvin Black, who was dancing in circles onstage, apparently inspired by something on his iPod. Ben screamed dramatically as Kelvin accidentally danced into him. Bud and a scruffy boy named Scooter Nemo, who had wild, uncombed hair, began screaming too.

"Save us from these roughhousing menfolk!" trilled Scooter.

"Cut it out!" I heard Delilah call. She was down front right in the thick of things, looking dignified in pleated khakis and a turquoise long-sleeved shirt.

When I caught sight of Delilah, I had a sudden flash of realization. These Drama Clubbers, ALL of them, must have taken part in more than one opening night set of Spin the Bottle.

Had Miranda Goetz ever had to kiss Chris Seligman? Had Ben Pfeiffer been commanded by the bottle to lock lips with Delilah Fortescue? Or with the leggy and glamorous Mia Kezdekian? If the bottle told Mia to kiss Scooter Nemo, would she do it? Would *I* do it?

Oh. The horror.

The buzz of activity came to an abrupt halt when a man walked up the stairs and stood center stage, waiting expectantly. He had to be Mr. Romeo. He had an air of authority about him, and I was amazed at the way so many people seemed to fall into an immediate and respectful silence, though Ben Pfeiffer continued to do his impression of an over-caffeinated grizzly bear.

I sat up straight, looking as attentive as possible. Having taken stock of everyone in the room, I could see that there were about eight other newbies at the meeting, a few of whom were sitting at the end of our row. One of them, the cherub-faced girl with blond ringlets I'd seen at the activities table, flashed me a wide smile. I pretended not to see. I might want to distance myself from these youngsters, particularly ones that looked like they belonged on a television commercial for peanut butter. It might not be good for my image to be seen palling around with them. Harper, of course, with her cool and calm demeanor, was different. And so was I. I had, after all, been studying my craft for years. My newbie status was only a technicality.

"Okay, people," Mr. Romeo called. "I'll need all of your attention now, please. We need to— Ben Pfeiffer!"

Ben froze, mid-caffeinated-bear-dance, hopped down off the stage, and found himself a seat.

Mr. Romeo was a slender wisp of a man with closely cropped silver hair and a kind of long Harry Potter–type scarf draped around his neck. He looked scrubbed and polished within an inch of his life. Not one hair was out of place. His clothes looked like they'd been pressed within the hour. I don't think I've ever seen a cleaner looking human being. If soap bubbles had floated out of his mouth when he opened it, I wouldn't have been a bit surprised.

"As I was saying, people, welcome all—particularly our new Drama Club members—to the auditions for our fall musical production, *Guys and Dolls*. I am Mr. Romeo, and I will be your director for this production. I presume that most of you are familiar with the show, so I'm not going to bore you with a long-winded synopsis of the plot."

I sat up even straighter, nodding vigorously to make it quite clear that I obviously knew a great deal about *Guys and Dolls*, and that I was thoroughly prepared for the audition in a way most newbies were not expected to be. In truth, I had spent ten minutes reading a plot and character rundown I'd found through Google last night. I had decided to audition for someone named Adelaide, because she seemed like she had some pizzazz.

"I hope you've all had sufficient time to review the handouts, which include monologues for each available role."

My stomach flipped.

I had been so absorbed in watching the old Drama Clubbers, I hadn't taken a single minute to read through the lines for the Adelaide audition. What was wrong with me? How had I let the local celebrities distract me from the task at hand?

"As usual, Miss Maslin will be our accompanist for both the rehearsal process and the production. If you are auditioning for a role that includes a musical solo, meaning the parts of Nathan, Sky, Sarah,

Adelaide, and Nicely Nicely, you'll do a line reading for me followed by a singing piece for Miss Maslin in the music room. Do *not* raise your hand to ask if the piece has to be from the show. Your musical piece does *not* have to be from the show. Sing whatever you want. If you can't think of anything, sing 'Jingle Bells.' We just need to hear your range, people."

The butterflies I had in my stomach turned into gigantic, genetically mutated Mexican jumping beans. With antlers.

"Now, before we begin, I'd like to see a show of hands from those of you who will be helping out with the production in some capacity other than performing."

Harper put her hand up. Down at the end of our row, a sleepy-looking guy in a Beatles T-shirt also raised his hand. Mr. Romeo peered over the tops of his glasses around the auditorium.

"Okay, hands down if I already know you. That leaves . . . let's see. Yes? You are?"

Mr. Romeo did not display bad manners by pointing. He simply gazed intently over his glasses at a seat while arching one silver eyebrow, and it was clear who he was talking to.

"Tyler Luddo, dude," said sleepy Beatles-shirt guy.

I was amazed anyone had the audacity to address

Mr. Romeo as "dude." I half expected a lightning bolt to scorch Tyler Luddo into bacon right where he sat.

"Tyler Luddodude," Mr. Romeo said, making a note on his clipboard. He spoke so crisply and professionally, it was hard to tell if he was being sarcastic or if he really thought *dude* was the last syllable of Tyler's name.

"And how would you like to contribute to this production?"

"Lights, stagehand work, you know. With my main man Scooter," Tyler replied. Scooter Nemo made a mild whooping sound.

"Very good," Mr. Romeo said, looking pleased. "Always important to have more hands backstage, and as always, people, I want to stress that the backstage work is *just* as important as what's happening under the lights."

Then Mr. Romeo nodded at Harper, who still had her hand up.

"Yes, and you are?"

"Harper Tanaka," she replied. "I'd like to be an assistant student producer. I can help out with designing the program, or doing publicity. Whatever needs to be done."

Harper was rewarded with a smile and a nod of approval.

"Excellent, Harper. Initiative and all-around enthusiasm. Watch and learn, people."

There were a few stifled snickers from undetermined areas as people turned around to look at Harper, but she simply tucked her hair behind her ears and looked straight ahead. The snickering died away. There's something about Harper that makes people suspect she doesn't care what they think. And, since she doesn't seem bothered by being mocked, there's no point in doing it.

"Let's get started then," Mr. Romeo stated, smoothing his hair into place in spite of the fact that it was already immaculate. "We'll go part by part, and I'd like to begin with Adelaide. Hands raised, please, if this is the role you intend to read for."

Yikes! Adelaide was first and I *still* hadn't looked at the lines. It was like one of those dreams I had about showing up to take a final exam in a class I'd forgotten to attend all year. I raised one hand, while quickly paging through the stapled handout with the other. Adelaide was on page two, and her speech was about twenty lines long. I looked around discreetly to see who else was going for the part.

Criminy! Miranda Goetz and Mia Kezdekian were BOTH raising their hands. Like I wasn't already nervous enough. I noticed the Blond Cherubic Newbie who had smiled at me was also raising her hand. That irritated me. Adelaide was a big part. This girl was only a seventh grader. A newbie. Whereas I . . . well, okay. I was those things too. But I was also different. I had passion. I had experience. I had . . . been to theater camp.

"Okay, Adelaide readers down front, please," Mr. Romeo called.

And I *still* hadn't looked at the stupid lines! Delilah had warned me against overthinking the lines, but surely she didn't mean not to read them at all.

I hissed a swear word at Harper. It was a cry for help.

"You're fine. You're *fine!*" she whispered, giving my arm a supportive squeeze, then nudging me to go.

So I got up and walked down the aisle to the Adelaide group, but I was decidedly *not* feeling good about it. In the fourth grade, Harper and I briefly explored the world of baking together, and we started baking cakes and things every day after school. Harper had told me that my first attempt at chocolate chip cookies was "fine," and she'd eaten four of them to prove it, even though I'd forgotten the sugar and put in twice too much baking soda. By *fine*, Harper really meant that I was not in danger of immediately dying or causing death to others.

There were six or seven in the little group besides

Mia and Miranda. I noticed with slight satisfaction that the Blond Cherubic Newbie looked as freaked out as I felt. Some of the girls chatted casually. Romalla Lee Um stood off to one side, towering over everyone else, looking lost in thought. The Blond Cherubic Newbie started to sidle over to me, but I ducked my head and pretended to be looking at the lines. Which gave me the perfect opportunity to *actually* look at them.

"Listen up. I'm going to call some names randomly, in no specific order," Mr. Romeo announced.

Duh, since random sort of does mean in no specific order. But I did some more ultra-serious nodding, because no actress in her right mind would let a director feel like he'd said something boneheaded.

"Miranda Goetz," he called. "Yes, why don't you start with Miss Maslin in the music room."

You still have time, I told myself. Read the lines again. And I tried to, though I kept stopping after the first line, to better contemplate my terror.

"And, let's see . . . you are?"

No. No. He could not be looking at *me*. He could *not* be talking to me. If I didn't look up, I wouldn't see him. If I didn't see him, he wasn't there. And if he wasn't there, he couldn't be calling my name. And if he wasn't calling my name—

"Yes? You are?" Mr. Romeo repeated.

Yes, I am. I met the gaze of those squeaky-clean eyeballs.

"Phoebe Hart," I whispered, using Real Acting to try to cover my misery and dismay.

"Very good," he said, like I got points for pronouncing my name correctly. "Whenever you're ready."

That was it? I was being thrust onto the stage with no pep talk? No helpful directorial suggestions? No privacy?

Because instead of resuming their chatting and horsing around, the collective eyes of the Drama Club, row of newbies included, were watching me expectantly. I swallowed, and it made a sound.

"Whenever you're ready," Mr. Romeo repeated, which by his tone obviously meant *Now would be a good time.*

I swallowed again, this time silently. Now I knew why there had been no auditions in elementary school. No ten-year-old could possibly survive this. When I started up the little staircase to go onstage, I was sure I was going to faint dead away. You're fine, I told myself. You are not in danger of immediately dying, or causing death to others. All you have to do is give a decent, animated, intelligent reading of twenty or thirty sentences.

I walked to the center of the stage, and raised the

paper. The silence in the auditorium was deafening. My hands were shaking. My feet were sweating. I took a deep breath.

"Nathan, where ya been?" I began.

Squeaky! Too squeaky! I took another generous breath, but before I could get the next word out, the side door near the seats flew open and someone ran in, calling "Sorry!" and skidding into a seat in the very front row.

No.

Way.

It was the OOMA, sitting not twenty feet away, looking at what everyone else was looking at. Which was me.

That, as they say, was the straw that broke the camel's back. I felt the world begin to tilt under my feet, and I turned and ran offstage, dropping the handout pages on the way. By some miracle there was a large garbage can just behind one of the flats. I sprinted to it and grabbed hold with both hands.

Then I threw up, loudly and burpingly, for all the Drama Club to hear.

CHAPTER FOUR

The Post-Vomitus Report

There is something permanently and life-alteringly disgusting about the reality of vomit.

Yes, everybody does it. But while we can look at the average person and not necessarily think about them throwing up, we can never look the same way at someone we once witnessed doing it. We will always, somehow, retain the image of half-digested liquid passing through their lips and into, say, a garbage can.

Now tell me. Would *you* ever consider putting your lips on a pair of lips you'd seen take a hot vomit shower?

I think not.

"Phoebe, don't overdramatize this," Harper was

saying as she perched on my bed fluffing my fat blue pillow.

"Overdramatize?" I shrieked, thrusting my hands in the air and flapping them around with furious emotion.

Okay, so she had a point.

"I'm so embarrassed," I said, putting my hands in my jeans pockets to stop them from gesticulating.

"I know," Harper said. "But if you really think about it, Pheebs, it was a simple digestive malfunction. A biological mishap. And since Mr. Romeo let you read for the part again in his office after everyone else was done, you didn't even blow the audition. In the long run, you didn't really lose anything."

Other than that one item.

"Okay, except your lunch," Harper added.

"I'm ruined," I moaned, sinking desolately into my vintage mid-1970s faux fur–covered beanbag chair.

"You aren't," Harper insisted, putting my blue pillow back where it was supposed to be.

"No seriously. Listen," I said, putting one hand on my hip, which is very hard to do in a beanbag chair. "I'm a victim of multiple traumas here. First we start a new school, filled with miniature grown-ups and new rules and strange systems. Then there's the arrival of the OOMA, which basically tilts my personal planet on its axis and totally messes with every cell in my brain."

Harper nodded to indicate she was still with me.

"Then we go to sign up for Drama Club, which I've been wanting to do for decades—"

"For years," Harper corrected.

"—for years, and find out there's a long-standing tradition in the club requiring participation in a very public game of Spin the Bottle."

Harper waited.

"The very implications of which are TERRIFYING," I added, to no visible effect. "And before I've had a chance to recover from all these things, I go to audition for my first show and experience a—what did you call it?"

"A digestive malfunction," Harper said gently.

"A digestive malfunction in front of Mr. Romeo and the ENTIRE Drama Club, including the Object of My Affection, who will obviously now be forever revolted by the mere mention of my name. Any chance I ever had of being a significant female person in the OOMA's life is completely destroyed."

"First of all, his name is Tucker," Harper said. She retrieved my blue pillow and cuddled it in her lap like a puppy.

"What? WHAT? How do you know that?" I spluttered.

"He was walking by with Kelvin Black when you were having the audition makeup and I was waiting for you," Harper said. "That's what Kelvin called him."

Learning the OOMA's name was far too much for me to process at the moment. I stared at Harper, delighted and enraged that she had seen the OOMA when I wasn't around.

"And you can't just make sweeping statements about your future like that," Harper continued. "You haven't even officially met the guy. Before the audition, the sum total of your relationship with him was making a strange noise and having your eyes bug out when he asked about his Frisbee."

"I know," I said. "But Harper, what if that was all it took? I'm telling you, I was just minding my own business one minute, and suddenly I'm struck down by Cupid's bow. I don't know how it happened. I don't know why—I think it was . . . Okay, I don't mean to be Cheese Central here, but I think it was when I saw his eyes. It was . . . They . . . What's that thing people say about the eyes . . . that they're the portal of . . . That they're the doorway to—"

"The eyes are the windows to the soul," Harper said.

"Exactly!" I shouted. "The windows to the soul.

You know me, Harp. I don't have a history of nutzoid behavior. But I think I kind of . . . saw his soul. And it was like one of those love at first sight things you hear about. I know it's not very scientific or anything, but I really believe it might be possible. 'Cause, you know, if there's such a thing as soul mates, wouldn't you recognize each other? Like, right away?"

"I believe in love at first sight," Harper said. "I believe in soul mates. My father has a friend whose field of research is the electromagnetic properties of the human psyche. It makes perfect sense to me that certain electric fields would be reactive with certain others, if the conditions were right. I'm not saying he might not be your soul mate. I'm saying you can't decide based on one incident that Tucker will never like you at all."

Harper surprises me sometimes. Like I keep saying, she's really smart. So when she believes in something as unscientific as soul mates or angelic intervention or the Loch Ness Monster, it gives it this kind of intellectual stamp of approval. And though she couldn't give me any advice about how to behave around a boy, her theories of electro-magnetic psyche thingies was pretty cool. Except that mine ended up being a lot more "reactive"—as Harper had put it—than I would have liked.

"I *threw up*, Harper," I said. "He came in, and he

saw me up onstage, and I ran away and threw up. It's really hard to erase something like that from a person's memory. The OOMA—Tucker is going to think I'm digestively unpredictable. And the rest of the Drama Club will write me off as a Nervous Nellie. My life is worse than anyone else's I know."

Harper swung her feet over the edge of the bed and stood up. Even though she's just as short as me, Harper has the ability to appear very tall sometimes. I stayed curled in the beanbag.

"Pheebs. If your life were actually worse than anyone else's, you wouldn't HAVE any of these problems. These problems are too GOOD. They mean you're out there experiencing the real world. Because you ARE in the Drama Club. Because you DID meet a boy who tilted your personal planet. Because you HAVE gone to your first audition. You've been talking about being in a real play since the fourth grade. You've actually met someone you are seriously thinking may be your soul mate. Those things don't make your life worse, they just make it more complicated. And complicated is GOOD."

Only my best friend could make me start believing that the worst day of my life should actually be celebrated with cake and singing. I played with part of the beanbag, beating an indentation in it, then squeezing all the little beans back into the dent.

"These are your salad days, Phoebe," Harper added, in what seemed to be her closing statement. Except for the sad but not unusual fact that I didn't know what she was talking about.

"My salad days?" I asked.

"Shakespeare," Harper said. "'My salad days, when I was green in judgment.' It's from *Antony and Cleopatra*. It means the time in your life when things are *supposed* to be this way. It's a learning process. Green signifies youth, and judgment comes through experience."

I sighed.

"In the big picture, Harper, I see what you're saying. I do. But that doesn't take away from the fact that right now, in this moment, I know that I've completely humiliated myself in front of people I wanted to impress. I just don't feel like I can face any of them. I definitely can't go back to school tomorrow."

Harper sat back down on my bed.

"You *have* to go to school tomorrow. They're posting the cast list. Besides, you have no legitimate reason not to go."

"Yes I do," I countered. I tried getting out of the chair because my legs were falling asleep. But it had molded itself around me, and now the entire thing had me in its grip. I finally submitted to the forces of gravity and stayed where I was.

"I do," I repeated. "I need a mental health day."

"There's no such thing," Harper said.

"There is too, and I need one. I have to create a buffer zone—let a little time elapse from the audition. Then it won't be so fresh in everyone's mind. I'll develop one of those twenty-four-hour things. Headache, sore throat, red itchy eyes."

"That's not a solution, Pheebs," Harper said. "Delaying the inevitable is not going to help. Remember in fourth grade when Billy Stilton got hit in the stomach with a basketball and accidentally wet his pants?"

"Of course I remember," I said.

"He didn't come back to school for three days after that," Harper said.

"I know," I replied. Poor Billy Stilton. I'm sorry to say it helped to remember that someone's life *was* worse than mine.

"So by the time he finally did show up, had we all forgotten about him peeing?" Harper asked.

I remember the whole thing like it happened yesterday. Rather than making us forget, the three days we'd had to contemplate and discuss Billy's accident probably made his ultimate return even worse.

"Okay, you have a point, Harp. But I actually am starting to feel a little ill. I'm pretty sure my head is throbbing."

Harper leaned forward and threw my favorite stuffed otter, Tonky Butt, right at my head.

"Hey!"

I was reaching for Tonky Butt to throw him back at Harper when I heard a knock. The door opened immediately, as is my mother's custom. She's always very careful about knocking, because of what she calls "privacy issues," but she never actually waits for a response. A person would certainly not have time to shout "Hang on a minute." It's like one of those cop shows where they shout "Police—open the door!" but by the end of the sentence they're already bursting into the house with splinters of wood raining down everywhere.

Did I mention my mother is a psychotherapist? Known in laymen's terms as a shrink? Known in daughter's terms as a bummer?

"Phoebe, you have a guest," my mother said. She was wearing her pale blue tracksuit, the one that, as would be momentarily evident when she turned to go, had "SMILE" printed in neon pink on the butt.

"Yes I know, Mom, Harper's been here for—"

But I shut right up when my mother stepped to one side and Delilah Fortescue, live and in the flesh, walked into my room.

Without the hat yanked down to her nose and in good light, Delilah Fortescue looked bigger than life. She wasn't drop-dead mysterious and stunning, like Mia Kezdekian. But she clearly had *something*. Tall enough to play tall, but convincingly able to play short. Pretty enough to play beautiful, but not so gorgeous she couldn't act plain. She was a fascinating mix. But mostly it was the way she carried herself. This was a person your eye was immediately drawn to, a person who didn't look like they felt flawed or unremarkable in any way.

Delilah walked into my room like she'd done it a thousand times, then smiled over her shoulder as she thanked my mother.

"You're very welcome, Delilah," my mother said. "A *great* pleasure to meet you."

I thanked the stars above that my mother was now leaving, rather than expounding on how our family had seen all of Delilah's star performances and how little Phoebe just idolized her. Sometimes my mother could be downright tactful. Which almost made up for the other times when she became a pathological life-ruiner.

I was trying to get out of the beanbag chair to properly greet Delilah. I mean, here she was in my *bedroom*. This girl who was like, famous. I needed to be standing. And yet here I was still stuck in the beanbag like a bug on its back, my limbs flailing uselessly. Harper suddenly appeared over me, reached down, grabbed my forearm, and pulled me up. My mouth opened and closed, as if I were a fish Harper had just pulled out of the water. The Outer Me had taken over. Harper looked at me, then turned to face Delilah.

"Hi," Harper said.

Once again, Harper had broken the speak-first spell.

"Hey, you're Harper, right?" Delilah asked.

Harper nodded.

"I'm sorry to barge in," Delilah said. "I just wanted to check on you, Phoebe. Now that I see you, you seem totally fine, but I was worried that you'd be stressing over what happened today. Some people might freak out over something like that, you know. Or just disappear."

I nodded. Yes. Yes to everything.

"I wanted to tell you these things happen to all of us sooner or later. Seriously, you have no idea what some of us have gone through. Auditions, opening night, understudies stepping in at the last minute. I'm telling you, we've *all* had something happen that was utterly mortifying. Once, I saw this audition by an actor who shall remain nameless, and he'd eaten the con carne chile for lunch, and right in the middle of it he cranked one out that was so loud you could hear it in the back row. Nobody thought twice about today, I can promise you that. I'm president of the Drama Club, after all, so I ought to know."

Delilah had taken both of my hands in hers and was staring at me intently with earnest, slightly bugged-out eyes. Her hair, pulled back in a high ponytail, bounced sympathetically as she nodded to emphasize what she'd just said. I tried to speak, only to discover the Outer Me was playing mouth commando with my lips. This was the second time it had happened even though Harper was right there.

"I vleh—you duzn't—vim—"

"I was just telling her the exact same thing," Harper interrupted, saving me from any further blahbbity speak. "See, Phoebe? There's nothing to worry about. It's fine."

I nodded, and since Delilah was still nodding, we looked like a pair of synchronized swimmers who'd just come up for air.

"It's fine," Delilah repeated. "Fine."

Fine. Meaning I was in no danger of immediately dying or causing death to another.

"And I heard you got to make up the audition later," Delilah added. "That's great! Because the cast list goes up tomorrow no matter what, so if you miss the audition, you're out of luck. That happened two years ago with this girl who got the hiccups. Seven hours straight. She just couldn't read her lines."

There was kind of a silence then. I didn't want to garble my words again, so I kept my mouth shut.

"So what time does the list get posted?" Harper asked after a moment.

"One o'clock sharp," Delilah said, her face shining with anticipation. "Right outside the main auditorium doors. It's nuts. Everyone crowds around, all going out of their heads with the suspense. Nobody ever really sleeps the night before. Which is tonight!"

"You're going to get Sarah," I said. A triumph of speech—I had gotten the words out without a hitch. "Everyone was saying so," I added. It was true. I'd overheard numerous people theorizing that Delilah would clinch the lead role.

Delilah blushed.

"I don't know," she said. "That would be really awesome, right? I'd love to play Sarah. We'll see. There was some pretty stiff competition today."

She said it convincingly while still managing to look like she knew she'd get the part. I was trying to muster up another complete sentence when Delilah came forward and gave me a big hug. All the air was expelled from my lungs as she squeezed.

"You're a sweetie," she said, then abruptly released me. "Promise you won't stress over today."

"I promise," I said, and I actually was starting to believe it. What was there to worry about now? Delilah Fortescue herself had come to see me. Actors who had come before me had cut the cheese or hic-cupped their way through auditions. I didn't need to worry about facing the others now.

Delilah clapped her hands in a solo burst of applause.

"Awesome," she said. "We're going to have a blast, girls. Listen, I've got to hop. Bud's waiting outside with our bikes. I'll see you both at one o'clock on the dot, right?"

I nodded grandly. As Delilah headed for the door, she turned and did the smiling over her shoulder thing.

"Good-bye!"

Harper raised her hand in kind of the same way the Pope does when he's blessing a whole crowd of people.

"Bye," I responded. Two seconds later Delilah had completed her exit, leaving only a flowery scent of perfume to prove she'd ever been in my room.

"Wow," I said, turning back to Harper, who'd already plopped down across my bed again.

"Yeah, really. What was she selling?"

"Selling?"

"I've never seen anyone be that effusive without having something they were trying to sell," Harper replied.

I was afraid to ask what effusive meant. It sounded like something that a zit might do.

"I thought that was incredibly nice of her to come by like that," I said.

Harper shrugged.

"Don't you think?" I continued. "You know, that it occurred to her I might be upset, and for her to go out of her way to come by and reassure me, and tell me about the guy who auditioned after eating chili and all that?"

"I guess you could look at it that way," Harper said. "Does this at least mean you've recovered from your twenty-four-hour flu?"

I grinned. "I have indeed, Harp. I'm feeling just fine now."

"Then we can change the subject. Because now that you've fully recovered . . ."

"Yes?"

Harper sat up and clasped her hands together.

"Will you do Mr. Romeo for me?"

Would I ever. I'd been dying to try ever since he'd walked into that audition. I ran to my closet and grabbed a long scarf my mother had produced in her brief knitting-for-therapy phase. I wrapped it around my neck, smoothed my frizzy red hair back, adjusted my imaginary glasses, and turned to face Harper.

"Peeeeeepuhl, pleeeze! Listen uuup!" I sang.

Harper giggled wildly.

"And yoooooooooouuuu are?" I asked, peering at Harper intently. "Excuse me, yes? And you aaaaaare?"

I grabbed a *People* magazine and pretended it was a clipboard.

"Ahhh, yes. Very good. Excellent."

Harper kept right on laughing. I had Mr. Romeo dead-on perfect, and I knew it. I *was* a good actress.

I felt perfectly happy for the first time that entire day.

Very good.

Excellent.

CHAPTER FIVE

The Cast

Harper had gone to see the principal to get special permission to attend the ninth-grade precalculus class, which was important to her intellectually, but also I suspect because it would get her out of gym. What this meant to me (in addition to the ugly specter of attending gym without her) was that I had to brave the cafeteria line myself. Harper had promised to find me as soon as her meeting was over, but she wasn't exactly sure when that would be. And I was hungry.

The seventh and eighth graders eat earliest in middle school, while the ninth graders had their own private time slot later. Maybe this avoided food fights or competition for the available beige or light green entrees, or maybe it was just because the cafeteria itself was so small.

Almost no one else was in line yet, so I pushed my tray along the counter, accepting a fish patty and something optimistically called "broccoli au gratin" from the lunch lady. I also grabbed a chocolate milk. I controlled my choices now that I was in middle school, and my choices involved chocolate whenever possible.

Since I was early, there weren't too many people seated in the cafeteria. This limited the number of eyes that could stare at me as I carried my tray to a back table. Harper thinks that the lingering memory of childhood cafeteria-oriented trauma accounts for at least one-third of all cases of adult-onset anxiety, and I have to agree. There just wasn't any easy way to get through a school lunch. Especially if your best friend was in the principal's office.

I sat in the corner at an empty table, and tried to focus on my food. I cut the fish patty in half, then cut it again into quarters. I pushed the broccoli around on the plate, where it left a little snail trail of white cheese behind it. Then I opened my chocolate milk and downed all eight ounces in a single gulp. Now that my taste buds were happy, I speared a hunk of fish patty and put it in my mouth. This is when my problems began.

Have you ever heard the expression "bitten off more than you can chew"? Well, there was about twice as much food in my mouth as there should have been. I tried to chew the fish patty while keeping my lips pressed together, but I could feel my cheeks bulging dangerously.

"This seat taken?"

I looked in the direction of the voice, and froze. The OOMA was standing several chairs away, holding a tray heavily laden with multiple beige and green selections and three milks. He was as stunning as I remembered, in a slightly rumpled pine green T-shirt and his usual faded jeans, a shock of black hair hanging over one eye.

I could not move. There was absolutely no available space in my mouth, so even trying to speak was impossible. If I resumed trying to chew to get the fish down, there was a good possibility some of it might be forced out of my mouth. So I just sat there like a world-class moron, my eyes bulging and my cheeks the size of baseballs, straining to contain the mush.

"I'll take that as a no," he said, giving me a slightly lopsided grin. He pulled up a chair, placed his tray on the table, and sat down.

"So," he continued breezily. "Ready to see that cast list?"

I tried to nod casually to buy time, but I could feel

my eyes filling with tears, and all that half-chewed fish patty was still trapped in my mouth and not going anywhere. If this wasn't worse than throwing up, it was definitely in the running. I was alone at a table with Tucker, your basic dream-come-true, and given the circumstances, there was only one thing I could think to do.

Flee.

I didn't even take my tray. I just jumped up from my chair, grabbed my bag, made a vague hand gesture at Tucker that was supposed to look something like "Oops I forgot I gotta go RIGHT NOW byc see you later," and sprinted out the side door to the hallway. I rushed straight for the staff/handicapped-accessible restroom that no one ever used, shooting through the door and locking it behind me.

This was one of the few bathrooms in school that had only one stall and an outside door that locked. I wasn't really supposed to be in it, but that was the least of my worries. I was temporarily safe. I grabbed the trash can, leaned over it, and opened my mouth. The hunk of half-chewed fish tumbled out. It landed in the can and lay there looking like an exhausted beige hockey puck. I grabbed some paper towels and covered it up.

Then I went to the sink and splashed cold water on my face, because that's what people seem to do when they need to snap out of a trauma. I put on some strawberry lip gloss that Harper had given me, because the scent was comforting. I did one of the calming breath sequences my mother had insisted I learn. Then I touched my toes a few times, because I didn't know how to do actual yoga, and this seemed like the next best thing. And then I took a good long look at myself in the mirror. I tried to see what the OOMA would have seen, without the mouth full of fish.

I would not say that I'm ugly. I really do not think I am. I actually don't think there are many truly ugly people in the world. There are a few, and they know who they are. I'm not one of them. As I've said before, I'm just flawed, and more or less unremarkable.

I've always thought an actress should have features that capture a person's attention. Not necessarily beautiful features, but strong ones. As I'd observed, Delilah Fortescue was not a gorgeous girl, but she was very noticeable. I was average from head to toes. Nothing about me stood out, not even my red hair, though Harper claimed it did. It was too frizzy to be an asset. I was a blend-in. People were always forgetting they'd met me before, when I remembered them perfectly. Even my parents' friends did that—and who forgets meeting their friends' kid?

The most frustrating thing about all this was

that I knew that the Inner Me, the real Phoebe, *was* memorable. Possibly even remarkable. I did great impressions, and I could almost always make Harper bend in half laughing—she always said I was the only person in the world who could make her laugh like that. I could memorize almost anything with very little effort. I was great at doing accents. I could sing pretty well. I could reproduce most animal sounds, from moos to hee-haws, so accurately, you'd think you were on safari in Kenya, or at least at the petting zoo. I could change my body language into anyone else's—give me thirty seconds and I'll give you an eighty-five-year-old lady with the hiccups, and you'll *believe* it. I had a talent, and that was pretty cool. But as I had just proven in the cafeteria in front of the OOMA, when Harper was not around, I bore all the hallmarks of a walking biological disaster.

And even if I hadn't humiliated myself two consecutive days in front of Tucker, what would he see in me anyway? If he spun the bottle and it pointed at me, would he be disappointed? Revolted? Or would he not even care, and just hope he got Mia Kezdekian the next time around?

Who was I kidding? I didn't even know how to kiss. I stared at my reflection, focusing on my lips. They were, not surprisingly, unremarkable. Mia Kezdekian had extraordinary, pillowy lips. Even

Harper's lips turned up naturally in a fetching smile. Mine looked like they'd been drawn on my face with a crayon as an afterthought. I puckered, closing my left eye all the way, but leaving the right one open a little so I could peek.

I began to lean toward the mirror, still puckering. One single hair had migrated in front of my face and was floating around, tickling my nose. I pushed it out of the way, then re-puckered and leaned in toward my own reflection. At the last moment, I decided it would be gross to actually put my lips on the bathroom mirror, so I slipped my right hand on the glass. And then I kissed it.

I suspect that if my hand had lips, it would tell me my kissing was not very good.

Even after I'd abandoned the kissing experiment, I stayed in the bathroom another ten minutes enjoying the solitude. Rather than do nothing, I got a jump on my math homework. When I looked at my watch, it was ten of one.

Now I wasn't sure how I felt about rushing over to the cast list posting. The OOMA would more than likely be there, after all. Why did I need to see the list right away? While I still had aspirations to stardom, I knew there were only two big female parts in the show. My second audition for Mr. Romeo and Miss

Maslin had definitely been decent. But there was a lot of competition for those two parts, and I was, technically, only a newbie. I might get a small part, one of the three- or four-liners, but there was more than a good chance I would end up in one of the choruses, and then I could only hope it was as one of the Hot Box Girls, rather than a member of the much duller Mission Choir group. I'd had it thoroughly drummed into me at Young Protégé Acting Camp that there were no small parts, and that if you couldn't hack being cast in the chorus, you didn't belong in the theater. Acting, we were told repeatedly, was a team effort.

And my team was the Drama Club. Delilah had as much as said she expected to see me when the list went up. How would it look if I didn't show up? No, I had to go, that was all there was to it. The question was, did I have enough time to find Harper first?

That problem, at least, was easily solved. I didn't get more than two steps out of the bathroom before I found Harper sitting on the floor by the cafeteria door, her math and social studies textbooks opened in front of her.

"What are you doing?" I asked her. Harper had started putting away her books when she saw me. She looked up again after zipping her bookbag closed.

"We were supposed to find each other at lunchtime. You weren't in the cafeteria, and I didn't know where else to look. I figured you'd come back and find me eventually. You mean to say you've been in the bathroom this whole time?"

"Yes," I said. "I mean, no. No! Well, yes, I was *in* the bathroom. But I haven't been, you know. Going to the bathroom."

"I get it," Harper said, getting to her feet. A blue foil wrapper from a roll of peppermint Life Savers drifted to the floor. Harper picked it up and put it in her pocket.

"Are you okay?" she asked.

I hesitated. Part of me wanted to blurt out the whole fish-patty-mouth-in-front-of-the-OOMA thing in excruciating detail. But it was complicated and embarrassing and I had done more than my fair share of complaining about my life to Harper in the last few days.

"I'm fine," I said.

"Then let's go."

We headed for the glassed-in breezeway that connected the cafeteria area to the auditorium area.

"How'd your meeting go?" I asked. Truth is, I had almost forgotten about Harper's precalculus thing. I had to be careful. If I got any more sucked into my own problems, even the usually unflappable Harper might take it personally.

"I'm in," she said. "The principal gave me permission."

"You'll miss gym," I told her, a little wistfully.

"Gym is for Tiny Minds," Harper replied.

I didn't bother pointing out that gym was a required class for us mere mental mortals, Tiny Minds or not. I could hear the sound of excited laughter and hooting ahead, and soon I could see that there was already a crowd near the auditorium doors. At the very moment Harper and I were approaching, Mr. Romeo came through the double doors. He was wearing a crimson scarf and a black suit. Even from a distance, I knew he had not a hair out of place. Mr. Romeo was clutching a piece of paper, and the crowd parted around him as if he were Moses. A very well-dressed, dapper Moses. With one dramatic movement he tacked the paper onto the bulletin board and slipped away without ever saying a word.

Harper and I hung back as the group surged in around the list. I heard shouts of "Yes!" and "Dude!" and "Sweet!"

"Do you want to go up there?" Harper asked. She looked at me for a moment. It was hard to read her expression. She seemed worried, in a motherly kind of way.

"I'm going to let it all die down a bit," I said.

I saw Delilah Fortescue emerge from the group, one hand pressed open to her collarbone.

"I can't believe it. I just can't believe it," she was repeating. The words could have meant anything, but I was betting from the excited flush on her cheeks she'd gotten cast as Sarah.

Delilah seemed to have one hand still stuck in the crowd, but then a person emerged holding on to it. It was Bud Gelcho, grinning from ear to ear. He raised Delilah's hand up in the air like she was a prizefighter. Ben Pfeiffer grabbed him by the back of the shirt.

"Dude, I can't see the list. What'd you get?"

"We got Sky and Sarah, bro," Bud said. Delilah continued to repeat that she could not believe it, but she had started to look like she believed it quite thoroughly.

More people were emerging from the crowd. I noticed the Blond Cherubic Newbie, and felt a flash of irritation that she had been in there with the older kids. Bud and Delilah headed toward the cafeteria, and suddenly the crowd had turned into fifteen people, then half that many. I noticed Chris Seligman and Ben Pfeiffer high-fiving each other as they walked away. And finally there were just a few stragglers left.

"I'm going in," I told Harper.

"Good luck," she said, frowning a little.

I walked over to the bulletin board, trying to look like I was just taking a casual stroll. The list was organized in order of the characters' appearances, so other than the parts I knew, it was hard to tell what was a big role and what might just be a walk-on. Sure enough, there was Delilah's name next to "Sergeant Sarah," and Bud's next to "Sky Masterson." Next, my eye fell on "Adelaide," and I was surprised to see the part had gone not to Miranda Goetz and her golden throat, but to the mysterious Mia Kezdekian. Chris Seligman had been cast as her fiancé, "Nathan Detroit." And Ben Pfeiffer had gotten someone or something called "Harry the Horse."

Then my eyes fell on my own name. I ran my finger across to the parts column. Mission Choir member. My heart sank. Not only had I failed to score even a tiny real part, I had been sent to the prim and proper ranks of the Salvation Army chorus. While the Hot Box Girls would probably get to do fun dance numbers in cute outfits, the Salvation Army Mission Choir was supposed to wear military-style uniforms and sing hymns. I had been relegated to the Siberia of *Guys and Dolls*.

Harper was calling my name, but I just wanted to see the rest of the list. There were three other members of the Mission Choir, plus the Mission

Choir Director/Lieutenant Agatha, which to my surprise was Miranda Goetz. Lt. Agatha was a pretty small part for such a pro. Miranda would have to demurely conduct "Faith of our Fathers," while Mia Kezdekian hammed it up in heels and a feather boa. The shame!

Then I heard a voice from directly behind me.

"Liver Lips!" it said cheerfully.

I froze. A person of the male persuasion had just called me Liver Lips to my back. Here it was—the first barfing crack. And the jerk didn't even have the nerve to say it to my face. I wanted to whirl around and confront him, but I was frozen in place. My lower Liver Lip began to quiver. Was he going to say something else, something even meaner?

The jerk took a step to the side to get a better view of the list. Now I could see his face.

Should I have been surprised that the person who had called me Liver Lips was the OOMA? He had, after all, now witnessed two unfortunate events related to my digestive system. He had seen too much. Spin the Bottle or not, Tucker wouldn't kiss me if I were the last girl on earth. He looked over at me like he was noticing me there for the first time.

"Hey. You ran off before. Are you okay? It's Phoebe, right? I couldn't forget all that wild red hair."

My mind worked furiously. Was this another insult? My hair was ridiculous and unflattering—it made me look like Ronald McDonald's little sister. But Tucker looked so friendly now. Still, he had just called me Liver Lips. Though I wasn't even fully certain what it meant, I knew I had never been called something that disgusting before.

"It's gonna be a good show," Tucker said, scanning the list. Then he looked at me and gave me a crooked smile. He had a dimple. An actual dimple on one side of his mouth.

I made a little wordless sound that could have been mmm-hmmm for yes, or mmmmm-mmmm, for I'm not sure. I couldn't commit to anything while the OOMA's behavior was so confusing and inconsistent. At least it was a response of some kind. Tucker gave the list one last glance, then looked at his watch.

"Oh man, I'm late again. Bio lab assigns cleanup duty for eighth graders, and they dock your grade if you blow it off. Gotta hop. Catch you later, Phoebe."

Say "Catch you later" back to him, I urged myself. Wait, no. Don't. It might sound way lame. Plus, he's a jerk. Theoretically.

As Tucker trudged away, I looked around for Harper, who was standing exactly where I'd left her.

She'd been there the whole time. I rushed toward her, my eyes growing wet. The OOMA had cruelly insulted me, then pleasantly passed the time of day. What kind of a nut job was he?

"I was trying to tell you Tucker was coming down the hall," Harper was saying anxiously. She fumbled in her pocket and produced the half-eaten roll of peppermint Life Savers and handed it to me—her cure-all. "Didn't you hear me trying to get your attention? You look upset! Is it the cast list? Is it Tucker? Phoebe, talk to me!"

Harper. Safe, adorable, non-Liver-Lipped Harper, who was lucky enough to not yet care about boys— grabbed both my hands and squeezed them.

"Pheebs, what's going on?"

I wanted to act it all out for Harper—make her laugh so I'd laugh about it too. I wanted to imitate myself with overstuffed cheeks full of fish patty. I wanted to demonstrate my make-out session with the bathroom mirror. I wanted to act out Tucker sneaking up behind me, calling me Liver Lips, and then going all multiple-personality-disorder.

Instead, I burst into tears.

CHAPTER SIX

Rehearsal

It didn't take Harper long to clear things up. She led me back to the cast list and pointed at the part Tucker had gotten.

The character's name was Liver Lips Louie.

Tucker had simply been reading the list out loud, NOT rudely and vilely insulting me. But that was three strikes for me—and I was out. Vomit, fish patty, and now the Liver Lips misunderstanding. I was a world-class idiot. Someone should have prepared us for how complicated middle school was going to be. They should have sent out a memo. Formed a support group.

My mother produced her usual bizarre reaction when I finally told her I'd been cast as a Mission

Choir member the following morning at breakfast.

"And?" she asked me, with her unique mother/ therapist tone. My father wisely stayed silent and hidden behind his *New York Times*.

"And what?"

She buttered a piece of toast and remained silent for a moment.

"And . . . how do you feel about that?"

I can't tell you how tired I'd become over the years being asked how I felt about something. Especially early in the morning, when no sane person knows how they feel about anything.

"I don't know, Mom, how do *you* think I should feel?" I shot back.

She gave me the classic raised eyebrow of a shrink in session. As I waited for her to say something, I wondered for the millionth time why she couldn't dye her hair instead of letting it go gray, and why she had to wear it in a ponytail with one of those cloth scrunchies you only saw in movies from the '80s.

"Do you feel you are expected to feel a certain way?" she asked.

I made an explosive sound of irritation, which only made her lean across the table toward me.

"Is there anything you want to talk about, Phoebe?" she asked very quietly.

What I wanted to do was rip the buttered toast

out of her hand and stick it to her forehead. But I knew from much experience that if I acted a) angry, b) sarcastic, or c) dismissive, she'd suspect there was indeed a problem and keep me there much longer, even if it made me late for school. And I wasn't about to be late when today was the first day of rehearsals. I might get detention or something, and miss it.

"Mom, I'm a seventh grader. It's not like I was expecting to be the lead in my first show. I'm not going to have a complex about it unless you give me one. So case closed, okay?"

And she let it go for the time being, but I knew Dr. Mom wasn't through with the subjects of Middle School, My Feelings, and the Mission Choir.

I made sure I got to rehearsal five minutes before the call time. There were about twenty-five chairs arranged in a large circle onstage. Harper, who had officially been named Student Assistant Producer, informed me that the first rehearsal was scheduled as a read-through, which I knew from theater camp meant the entire script would be read from beginning to end with no direction or comments. That meant that even people with little bitty parts at the very beginning or the very end of the show were expected to sit through the entire thing. Harper said she'd been asked to take down notes Mr. Romeo dictated to her, and help create a rehearsal schedule for the next four weeks.

Since no one had taken a seat up onstage yet, I hung back in the auditorium, watching. I thought it might look stupid to be the first to sit down. Usually I would just stick next to Harper, but she was having some sort of discussion with Miss Maslin that involved a clipboard and a calculator. So instead, I slouched in an auditorium seat and watched the goings-on. Ben Pfeiffer had gotten hold of Fedora Kravitz's purse, and was prancing around with it slung over his shoulder while Fedora shouted at him to give it back. Delilah and Bud were standing way down front, receiving compliments and good wishes gracefully from their castmates. I noticed Delilah had a hand firmly planted on Bud's back.

Behind me, I heard someone sigh sarcastically. I looked around discreetly, trying to look like I was merely stretching my neck. A person had sat down in the seat in back of me, hunched way down, feet propped up. Even though I didn't look directly at her, I recognized Mia Kezdekian right away. She was kind of unmistakable.

"That girl," Mia said, staring up at the ceiling, "is under the impression that this is the Shubert Theatre, and that she is Carol Channing."

I was confused. Not about the Shubert Theatre

and Carol Channing—I knew my theater legends backwards and forwards—but about who Mia was talking to. Because she wasn't looking at me. She was still staring up into space. But there wasn't anyone else within earshot. Could she be on one of those teeny-tiny headsets some people get for their cell phones?

I glanced back at her again. Yikes, the girl was even more of a major babe close up! She had jet-black glossy hair that hung straight down around her face, enormous blue-green eyes, and lips you could balance a pencil on. She was mesmerizing. Suddenly she lowered her head and fixed her eyes on me.

"You're one of the new kids," she stated.

I nodded. "I'm the one who threw up during auditions."

Why? Why? Why did I volunteer that?

"What's your name?"

"Phoebe Hart. I'm a Mission Choir member."

Translate: *Phoebe Hart. I'm a vomiting loser.*

"Right. Listen, Phoebe, be careful of that one," Mia said, gesturing toward the stage with a perfectly slim and elegant hand.

I couldn't believe she was continuing to speak to me after my two lame comments.

"Of which one?"

Still lame.

"Lady D up there."

"Delilah? Why?"

Mia shook her head.

"Just watch your back around her. Mr. Romeo thinks she's the greatest actress of all time. He casts her every year in a huge part. He thinks she can do no wrong. You won't believe the stuff she pulls, and he never says a word. She's like, the ugly stepsister. Gets everything, deserves squat."

I hadn't realized there was bad blood between Monroe's two ninth-grade starlets. Was I betraying Delilah by talking to Mia? I was suddenly torn between feeling defensive of Delilah and thrilled at finding myself in a real Drama Club drama. I nodded at Mia, but I began gathering my things together as if I were going to get up and leave. If Delilah saw me talking to Mia, she might get mad at me. Or think we were talking about her. Which we kind of were.

"Miranda Goetz got Mission Choir Director, right?" Mia asked, ignoring the fact that I'd stood up and started to move toward the aisle.

I paused and nodded again, then furtively peeked around to see if Delilah was looking. She was sitting on the edge of the stage with Bud, their heads bent over a script. She now had one hand squeezing Bud's arm. She hadn't noticed me talking to Mia, apparently. I inched back a bit, trying to place my body between Mia and Delilah's line of sight. Because to be honest, I was still kind of amazed and flattered that Mia was bothering to talk to me.

"Pay attention to Miranda's lines, learn them if you can. And watch what blocking they give her," Mia said. "Miranda's having major issues with her voice right now. Rumor has it she might have nodes on her vocal cords, which would mean surgery. If that happens soon, someone will have to step into her part. Someone who currently is in the chorus, but is able to make the leap."

"Me?" I squeaked.

Like a mouse. Asking for cheese.

The shame.

"It would make the most sense for it to be one of the Mission Choir members. You'll already have the Salvation Army costume. You'll already be familiar with the scenes. There's only, what? Three or four of you in that chorus? I'm just saying, be prepared. If the opportunity presents itself, and you just happen to have the lines and blocking memorized, you'll get the part."

"Wow . . . I . . . If . . . I mean, thank you for the heads-up," I stammered.

Mia shrugged.

"Why me? Sorry, I mean, how come you're telling me all this?"

Mia began braiding a lock of her hair. She still didn't look directly at me.

"Just because, that's all. I'm helping you out, Fiji, because I'm a nice person. And I'm sure you'll remember that."

So many thoughts went through my brain. The first was that my name wasn't Fiji, but the second was gratitude that Mia had singled me out about the possibility of a bigger part opening up. Though it was hard to think of her just being . . . nice. Goddess, maybe. Terrifyingly intimidating, possibly. But nice?

"People, listen up!" Mr. Romeo called. Mr. Romeo didn't seem to be able to make his voice very loud, so to compensate, he just raised it an octave when he needed everyone's attention. I was glad of the opportunity to look away from Mia and give my attention to our director. Mr. Romeo looked especially immaculate today. I could see the crisp creases in his pants and the high shine on his shoes five rows away. With his slender build and perfectly combed gray hair, he reminded me of a silver fox. He pursed his lips as he waited for everyone to quiet down, raising his chin as his glasses slipped just slightly down his nose.

"Time is short, people, and we've got to get this run-through started. Go ahead and take a seat onstage. If you have a scene partner, try to sit next to them. I'd like everybody seated and ready to go in one minute!"

He clapped his hands together twice to emphasize his instructions, and might as well have pulled a reverse fire alarm, the way people were suddenly scrambling over each other to grab seats. I noticed Mia Kezdekian climbing the stairs to the stage, and wondered how she'd gotten out of her seat and down the aisle without me even noticing it. More of what made her mysterious, I suppose.

I took a seat between Fedora Kravitz, who'd reclaimed her purse from Ben, and the Blond Cherubic Newbie, who beamed at me. She just didn't seem to get the message. I know that doesn't sound all that nice, but I didn't want a newbie as a friend. Delilah had singled me out, and now so, apparently, had Mia Kezdekian. So I had already set myself apart from the other seventh graders. I wasn't like them. I had studied acting. I had gone to Young Protégé Acting Camp. I didn't need amateur seventh-grade friends. Harper, of course, was different. I pretended not to notice the BCN's smile, and turned in Fedora's direction, watching with interest as she tied her wild, curly hair into a pulled-back knot. I had never seen anyone use their own hair as a scrunchie before. I made a mental note to mention this to my mom.

Almost all the seats seemed to be taken, and people were flipping through their scripts, some like Chris Seligman studiously highlighting their lines in yellow marker. The fact that he hadn't done it before now made it seem a bit showy, since his part was so big. I was acutely aware of the fact that the OOMA was not there. Liver Lips Louie had lines and everything. Where was he?

I tried to focus on the script. The story of *Guys and Dolls* follows two couples: Adelaide, the night club singer who has been waiting lo these fourteen years for her fiancé, Nathan, to set a wedding date; and the prim Salvation Army Sergeant Sarah Brown, who, against her better judgment, falls for the chronic gambler but golden-hearted Sky Masterson. The women are trying to change the men, and the men are trying to keep things the way they are, and somehow everything comes down to one huge dice game called "shooting craps," where everyone's future will be decided once and for all. Or something.

I fully intended to throw myself into the show heart and soul. But deep down, I was a little disappointed with the play. It was kind of old-timey and dated. I had been sort of hoping my first show would be more modern, and hip. Like *Rent*, maybe. But this was the show we were doing, and according to Mr. Romeo, it was one of the most popular revival shows in the country. Who was I to argue with the masses?

We started at the top of the show, and by page two I already had something to do. The Mission Choir, led by Mission Choir Director Lieutenant Agatha (aka Miranda Goetz) entered almost immediately in full Salvation Army mode, piously singing a hymn. Since we weren't starting song rehearsal until tomorrow, Mr. Romeo told us to just speak the song lines, but in the rhythm we would sing them. It was embarrassing, but I was determined to give it my all.

"Follow the fold and straaaaaaaaaaaay no more, straaaaaaaaaaay no more, straaaaaaaaaaaaaaaaay no more. Put down the bottle and we'll saaaaaaaaaay no more, follow, follow the fooooooooooooooold."

It was at this moment that the back door of the auditorium flew open, and the OOMA came trotting down the aisle.

"Sorry!" he called, tossing his bookbag onto a seat, and bounding up onto the stage.

I shot a quick look at Mr. Romeo, who appeared to be shooting sparkling lightning bolts from his eyeballs in Tucker's direction.

"Mr. Wells. As you are aware, I have a very low tolerance for tardiness."

"Sorry," Tucker repeated with his lopsided smile. He had taken a seat and had his script out and open, as if he'd been there all along.

There was a long pause, during which Mr. Romeo

seemed to be contemplating whether or not to eject Tucker from the universe.

"Top of page two again, please," he said at last.

I was relieved that Tucker had been spared, but not too thrilled to go back to the beginning of "Follow the Fold." We sounded like a bunch of witches calling up a tree spirit, but I did it, and I'm proud to say Mr. Romeo gave me a little appreciative nod at the end. Delilah had lines in this scene, which she read without too much energy. But Mr. Romeo uttered a quiet "Nicely done," so it must have been okay.

What I didn't expect was that when her scene was over and her character offstage, Delilah would have the nerve to pick up a book and start reading. I discreetly looked around at the other faces, but no one, including Mr. Romeo, seemed to notice what Delilah was doing, or care. Harper appeared to be writing furiously, making notes on her copy of the script. Tucker was leaning over to help retrieve the contents of Annabelle Peterson's purse, which had dumped out all over the floor, making me wish it was my purse that had ejected its contents. Nobody was looking at Delilah, except for Mia Kezdekian, who scrunched up her face and rolled her eyes. Maybe she was right about Mr. Romeo thinking Delilah could do no wrong. The nuttiest thing was the title of the book Delilah was so entranced in: *How Not to Look Fat*. I kid you not. Check Amazon.com.

It wasn't just a momentary thing either. Delilah read until one page before her next scene. She seemed to have some sort of magical inner guidance system that prompted her when one of her entrances was approaching. I especially noticed this because as a Mission Choir member, almost all of my scenes had Delilah in them, though she had a lot without us. I had started to feel a little irritated that Delilah wasn't paying more attention, when she suddenly put the book on her lap and gave me one of her big winks, like we were sharing a secret. I smiled at her. It wasn't that big of a deal, after all. Delilah had done tons of read-throughs, and she knew her part, and if she wanted to do a little nutrition-based reading between her scenes, what was wrong with that?

The whole read-through took a long time, and because of where Tucker was sitting, it was impossible for me to steal glimpses of him without leaning way forward in my seat and looking like the Queen of Lame. I had to be content with merely knowing he was sitting a few seats away, and occasionally hearing him read a line or two. When we got to the last line of the last page, everybody clapped and hooted for themselves and each other. Ben Pfeiffer leaped around the circle high-fiving anyone who'd let him.

I decided Ben Pfeiffer would high-five a wall if there was no person available. Mr. Romeo indulged this celebration for a few minutes, then sent his voice into a majorly soprano zone to retake control of the room.

"All right, people, all right now. Let's settle down please. PEOPLE!"

This last *people* reached the ears of Ben Pfeiffer, who high-fived one last dude before sitting down.

"Thank you. All right. Now, first of all, congratulations to each and every one of you on an excellent read-through."

The clapping and cheering exploded again, but Mr. Romeo anticipated it and raised his hand like Obi-Wan Kenobi. The room instantly fell silent.

"That said, people, we have an enormous amount of work to do. An *enormous* amount. As you know, with the second round of mandatory state testing that has been added into the curriculum, we've been forced to schedule our fall production a week earlier than last year. That gives us only *five* weeks, people, to stage this show, get off book, and get costumes and sets finalized. *Five* weeks!"

There were groans of disbelief coming from every direction. It did seem kind of insane. Five weeks from now we had to be ready for an audience.

"A great deal will be expected of you," Mr. Romeo

continued. Since everyone had gotten so quiet, his voice had dropped down to its original octave. "We may be in middle school, but we do things *professionally* here at Monroe. That means that when I say you have to be off book, I expect you to be off book. Some of you have a lot of lines, and you'll have to start work immediately if you're going to memorize them in time. In addition, we will have rehearsals scheduled on every school day, and if your name is listed on the rehearsal schedule, you are *required* to attend."

A little murmur went around the room. I noticed that the younger the student, the more intently they listened to Mr. Romeo. The Blond Cherubic Newbie, for example, was leaning forward gazing at him, her brow furrowed in an expression that screamed "I am listening to you with excessive concentration!"

I thought the BCN was going a little over the top, but I wanted to make sure Mr. Romeo knew I was paying close attention too. Since the furrowed brow thing was already taken, I chose to sit up very straight with the eraser end of my pencil in my mouth and nod visibly at choice moments during the talk.

"Also, people, let me remind you of something. Participation in the Drama Club does not excuse you from any scholastic commitments. The work you will do in this musical is in addition to and on top of any and all work you are assigned in class. Do *not* tell a teacher that you failed to complete an assignment because you were rehearsing late. Your excuse will *not* be accepted. That said, I understand that some of you may want to rethink your participation in *Guys and Dolls* at this point. Now is your chance, people. If you feel that you will not be able to function professionally in this production while simultaneously maintaining your academic commitments, let me know right now, and you will be permitted to drop out of the production with no penalty or bad feelings. It will not affect your status as a full Drama Club member, and none of us here will hold it against you. Anyone?"

Everyone looked around. Not a single hand was raised.

We had been warned that it would be tough going, and yet we were all in. I felt a sudden thrill of a shared burden, as if I were a member of a Navy SEALS team preparing to embark on a dangerous and brutal mission that involved great feats of human strength, sleep deprivation, and long periods without food or water.

"All rightee then," Mr. Romeo said. He looked pleased. A few people started to get up, but Mr. Romeo raised the Obi-Wan Kenobi hand.

"One last thing. I've been advised by the health office that several isolated cases of chicken pox have been diagnosed in the student body. At least one of those cases is in a student who had previously been vaccinated against the disease. It's my understanding that these vaccinations are not a sure preventative. Only people who have had a case of the chicken pox in the past are now fully immune. May I ask how many of you have *not* had the chicken pox?"

I raised my hand a little. So did Delilah, and Tyler Luddo. I could tell there were at least five or six other hands up, but I looked down. Checking to see who else was poxless seemed rude. I did glance over at Harper, who looked positively alarmed. Infectious diseases freak Harper out like being in middle school does for me. An infectious disease IN middle school provided Harper and me with an interesting area of common freak-out ground.

"All right, not too many of you. However. Chicken pox is contagious. Be vigilant, people. This is a team effort, and we need a *healthy* team. Stay healthy."

I nodded so hard, one of my earrings fell out. I caught it and put it back in, and nodded one more time for good measure. It was a strange thing to promise someone that you would *not* get a contagious disease, but I was promising Mr. Romeo, and I meant it.

I had a note from my mother allowing me to go home with Harper. I was glad today's read-through had been scheduled to end before bus departure. That meant I got to take Harper's bus home, which

I loved. Getting on someone else's school bus is like trying on someone else's life. It's familiar, but lots of little things are different. You get to see how other people live.

Harper was going over a stack of music sheets with Miss Maslin. She finished as I walked over to her.

"Hey, we better book if we're going to make the bus," Harper said. She had a tiny smudge of ink over her lip that made her look even smarter than usual, in an unkempt, nutty professor sort of way.

"I'm ready," I said, slinging my bookbag over one shoulder.

"Got your permission note?" she asked, all efficiency as we made our way to the auditorium door.

"Got my permission note," I confirmed.

Harper opened the door and waved me through ahead of her.

When I stepped out into the hallway, I turned and took another look at the stage, where just a few students were still milling around Mr. Romeo. I saw the rows and rows of seats, mostly empty.

And though every rehearsal would bring me one day closer to the unknown terrors of Spin the Bottle, I have to say, for the moment I was psyched. Anything could happen. Anything at all.

They don't call it drama for nothing.

CHAPTER SEVEN

If You're in the Play, You Gotta Play

I've spent more hours at Harper's house than I can count. She comes over to my house too, but I like it better at Harper's. It's more relaxed there, more free. At my house, I always get the idea my mother is hyperaware of everything we're doing and saying, in a mother/therapist-on-caffeine kind of way. And then when we come downstairs for a snack or something, she wants to "talk" to us. My father is usually still at work in his law office, so it's just Mom and us, which can feel like being a guest on *Oprah*.

Harper's house feels more like camp, without the tents. Her dad is a quantum physicist, which is a five-syllable name for math/science genius. He has an office at the local university, but he wanders home a lot. And Harper's mom is a painter. Seriously. You'll walk in the door and she'll be there in, like, a paint-covered old shirt and her hair wrapped up in a bandanna and a smear of indigo blue on her earlobe.

I've never known anyone else's mother to be so thoroughly and consistently thrilled when I walk through the door. Her whole face breaks into this huge grin, and she goes "Pheebers!" Then she zooms in for the hug. Which I used to try to duck out of, because it seemed embarrassing and because I didn't want indigo blue on *me*. But now I just let her because it's easier, because I like the way the paint smells, and because it's actually kind of nice.

Their food tastes better than at my house too. Harper's dad is Japanese, and some of his family recipes have left me close to tears of joy. The best was when I slept over, because we got to eat rice for breakfast, which everyone should try. I'm all for Cap'n Crunch, but the occasional bowl of hot rice in the morning can really give a person a new outlook.

I wasn't sleeping over tonight, though. My mother had late office hours that day, and she was going to pick me up at some specified time later. I planned to do my homework with Harper, because it was more fun that way and I always did better work when I was with her.

"Should we go up to my room?" Harper asked.

She was holding a bowl of dried wasabe peas and soy nuts that her mother had handed her before getting back to her painting.

"Have fun, girls, and come down to the studio if you get bored. I'm in a creative blitz!"

I loved visiting the studio, but I also wanted to get to Harper's room. I had a lot of homework, and I also wanted to talk about the rehearsal. I followed Harper up the worn, creaky stairs and down the narrow upstairs hall that was lined in bookcases. There were books everywhere in this house, even in piles on the stairs. Depending on the state of things, sometimes Harper's house looked more like a flea market than a place people lived. I loved it. While my mother believed in decorative unity (which means the curtains match the bedspread and the carpet and the lampshades and the garbage can), Harper's parents believed in a more free-for-all style.

The funny part was walking from the hallway into Harper's room. It was like entering another universe. The rest of the house was like a jumble shop of books and curiosities, but Harper's room was organized and tidied within an inch of its life.

"Did you bring the bio worksheet?" Harper asked.

I had a history of forgetting worksheets.

I nodded. But I let my bookbag sit untouched where I'd tossed it by the plaster cast of an elephant's footprint.

"So did you see who was talking to me at rehearsal? Before rehearsal?" I asked.

"No," Harper replied. She was sitting at her desk pulling her books out of her bag one at a time, and arranging them in front of her.

"Mia Kezdekian. She just started chatting with me out of nowhere."

Harper's basset hound, Newton, padded into the room, his ears swinging gravely. He trotted over to Harper, gave her an interested sniff, then collapsed at her feet into a deep and immediate sleep.

"I wish I could fall asleep that easily," Harper said, massaging the dog's round belly with her foot.

"Harper—seriously. Mia Kezdekian!"

"Pheebs, so what? You're in the Drama Club, she's in the Drama Club. You were sitting near her. She opened her mouth and spoke. What's the big deal?"

It annoyed me that Harper wasn't impressed.

"You won't believe what she told me."

Harper gave me a look that indicated she probably would.

"She told me to *watch my back* around Delilah Fortescue!"

Harper leaned down and readjusted Newton's collar, tucking his huge ears underneath it, then freeing them.

"Harper, I think they're like, enemies or something!"

"And this matters in any microscopic way because . . . "

"Well, Delilah reached out to me. You know. She actually came to my house, remember?"

"I come to your house all the time," Harper said, folding her arms. Newton snored at her feet, blissfully ignorant.

"I know, but it was like she was kind of indicating that she wanted to be my friend. Which is huge."

Harper made an irritated sound by blowing air out through her nose.

"Why? Why is it huge?"

"Because! Delilah is . . . you know."

"I'm afraid I don't, Phoebe."

"Delilah is a big deal. She's the president of the Drama Club!"

"So?" Harper frowned and leaned forward, tucking Newton's ears back under his collar.

"So, it's meaningful when she acts in a friendly way to some green seventh grader who's just starting out. I mean, you know. I felt kind of honored."

"If you say so," Harper said. But she didn't look

at me. She just kept fiddling with her dog's ears.

I was starting to get frustrated at Harper's apparent lack of interest, but I wanted to tell the story.

"So the fact that Mia then kind of makes nice with me too, I mean, do you think that's weird?"

The expression on Harper's face told me that she didn't much care.

"But wait, because listen to what Mia was telling me. I was getting up to leave, right? Because I didn't want Delilah to see me sitting there yakking away with Mia, who she apparently hates, but Mia keeps talking. And she told me that Miranda Goetz is having some sort of problem with her vocal cords, and if it gets worse she might not be able to be in the show!"

I leaned forward and lowered my voice to a whisper.

"She said I might want to think about learning Miranda's lines . . . you know. *In case.*"

"Why are you whispering?"

"Because I'm telling you a secret."

Harper drew her feet up underneath her.

"No offense, Pheebs, but it can't be that much of a secret at this point. I mean, if *we're* in on it. We don't even know Miranda."

I loved Harper to death, but she seemed intent on ruining *everything* today.

"I just think it's all rather interesting," I said. "And you know. Why would Mia pick *me* to tell these things to? Why would she tell *me* to learn Miranda's lines? Why not tell that Blond Cherubic Newbie girl?"

"Do we know she didn't?" Harper asked. "Do we know she didn't have this same conversation with every member of the Drama Club?"

"Well, she didn't have it with *you*," I said testily.

"No," Harper replied. "She didn't."

So now I felt bad.

"I'm sorry. It's just every time I get to talking about something interesting you kind of shut me down. I mean, why did you even join Drama Club?"

"Because *you* asked me to," Harper said quietly. "Because you really wanted to do it, but you didn't want to do it by yourself."

Ouch. Newton let out a little sleep groan, like he felt it too.

"I'm sorry," I said. "I wanted us to do it together. I thought we'd have fun."

"Because you don't like doing things by yourself," Harper said. "It's okay, you know. I don't mind. And I guess maybe we might potentially have fun. But you have to stop the prevalence of celebrity-obsessed culture from influencing your behavior in this way."

"The what?"

"These girls, Phoebe. Delilah and Mia and the rest.

They're *people*. You're talking about them like they're so important that if one of them deigns to talk to you it's this huge deal—that it makes *you* important too. The only difference between them and you is age, and maybe a little experience. Ever since seventh grade started, you've been putting people on pedestals and dancing around them like some kind of idol worshiper. Even Tucker is, at the end of the day, just a carbon-based life-form walking upright on two legs, like the rest of us."

I had been getting more than a little irritated as Harper lectured me, but when she brought up the OOMA, I sighed. I'd been bursting to talk about him, and Harper was the only one I could talk to. So I swallowed my anger.

"Oh, Harp, about Tucker. Can you believe he was late to rehearsal? I swear, I thought Mr. Romeo was going to fire him or something. I was so worried! Weren't you?"

"No," Harper said. "What I'm worried about is the outbreak of chicken pox at school. Do you know that if you get chicken pox, you're much more likely to develop shingles as an adult? Do you realize what a serious disease that can be? Studies are showing that a lot of chicken pox inoculations were ineffective. I got vaccinated, and I could get sick anyway. What other vaccines are going to turn out to be ineffective? That's what I'm worried about. And frankly, I was kind of hoping you'd help me get my mind off it. I just want to have a good laugh and get our homework done. I don't want to get chicken pox, and I don't want to get all mired down in Drama Club drama."

"Okay," I said carefully. "Sure. I've actually been working on a funny accent. It's the ninth-grade French teacher's. You know him? He's the one who walks with his chest stuck way out and his fists balled up? But let me just finish what I was saying first. What was I saying . . . ? Oh! The thing that keeps obsessing me, Harper, is I'm going to be forced to play Spin the Bottle with Tucker!"

Harper shrugged, her expression cool.

"Harper, come on! Why are you acting like you're so above all of this? Aren't you the tiniest bit nervous about it?"

"About what?"

"Playing the game, Harper! The opening night tradition of Spin the Bottle. I mean, I realize I probably think about it too much, but don't you ever think about it at all?"

"Not really, Phoebe. I don't really need to, since I'm not going to play."

Not play? It had never, not once, occurred to me that Harper would refuse to play.

"Not . . . Not . . . But Harper, you *have* to!"

Harper leaned down and rolled Newton onto his back. He accepted the tummy rub she gave him without appearing to wake.

"Why would you think that?" Harper asked.

I made an exasperated, explosive sound that woke Newton.

"Because it's like, required. It's tradition."

"So was sacrificing small animals to pagan gods, Phoebe, but somewhere along the line most people decided to stop doing it."

"But everybody is going to do it. Everybody has to. That's what Delilah said. If you're in the play, you gotta play."

"Not me," Harper said smoothly. "And technically, I'm not *in* the play. But even if I were, it wouldn't make a difference. I'm not interested in Spin the Bottle. Besides, do you have any idea what kind of bacteria and germs you expose yourself to when you play that game? You might as well just ASK to be infected with a cold, with chicken pox, with mono. It's like kissing a Petri dish in an infectious disease lab. No thank you."

I wanted to sail through the air like a ninja and throttle my best friend.

"I don't understand. Where is this coming from?"

"It's coming from an *individual*, Phoebe. I am

required to go to study hall. I am required to have my parents sign my report card. But I am not required to play Spin the Bottle. Nobody is required to, no matter what Delilah Fortescue or anyone says or thinks. This is what I'm trying to get across to you."

I scowled.

"I didn't realize how pathetic you thought it all was."

"I didn't say I thought it was pathetic. I understand how some people might want to do it. I understand why you would want to do it, Pheebs, given the Tucker situation. I just wish you'd stop pretending that you're being *forced* into it when you're not. You've been dying of curiosity about Spin the Bottle ever since you heard about the tradition. That's fine. But please at least admit to yourself that this is something you *want* to do. I know you, Phoebe. You're not a 'they're all jumping off a bridge so I've got to do it too' kind of a girl. At least you never were. You're authentic. So act like it."

I was so angry by now I could barely contain myself. She *said* she didn't think it was pathetic, but it was so obvious that she *did* think exactly that. Where was all this superiority coming from?

"Okay, fine, I do want to play!" I yelled, and I actually stomped my foot.

"I know you do. And I'm glad you know you do.

Now don't be mad at me just because I *don't*."

But I *was* mad. I was furious. How dare Harper *not* want to play Spin the Bottle? And how dare she *not* see that to be singled out by Delilah Fortescue made me special? We had always stuck together before. I had taken chess lessons with Harper in sixth grade, even though I stunk at it. Harper had joined Drama Club, even though it was my thing. We were Calvin and Hobbes. Snoopy and Woodstock. Why did Harper have to go and change all of that now?

"You know what, Harper?" I said, my voice shaking as I stood up. "You're obviously way too mature for my company. I don't think I ought to waste any more of your precious, genius time with my little baby hero worship stuff. I mean, maybe you have more *important* things to do."

Harper raised her chin and stared at me defiantly.

"Maybe I do," she said.

And though we were stuck in the same house until my mother picked me up, neither of us spoke to the other again that day.

CHAPTER EIGHT

Work Party

I had never had a fight with Harper before. I was literally sick about it —I couldn't put anything in my stomach for the next entire day. Sure, we'd squabbled over plot lines to our comic strips, and over which movies to rent on sleep-over nights, but never anything REAL. This fight was absolutely, unflinchingly real. After a very uncomfortable and silent hour following the argument, my mother had come by to pick me up. Harper had not called me that night, and I had not called her.

I wanted to. Really badly. I'd gotten several digits into dialing once, before hanging up. If she had called me, I would have overwhelmed her with my remorse and kindness. But there was no way *I* was going to call *her*. To call was to apologize, and I was sorry. I just didn't want to be sorry *first*.

In addition to leaving me feeling miserable and unable to eat, other fallout from the fight was that I would have to go alone to the "voluntary" Saturday afternoon work party for the *Guys and Dolls* set. I never would have signed up if I'd known Harper wouldn't be with me, but it was too late to go back and change it.

I'd always had a special dread of showing up to do something when I'd never done it before and didn't know what it was going to be like. The Outer Me could never act the way the Inner Me wanted her to. I always ended up spazzing. I'd actually had this glimmer of hope that Harper might just show up at the work party. Like out of the blue. To show that even though we were in a fight, she would never abandon me that way. But her mother called my mother to say Harper had decided to tag along with her father when he presented a paper on string theory at the university. I had to pretend like I already knew that, because I didn't want my mother to start asking questions about me and Harper. I probably would have burst into tears.

I showed up in baggy denim overalls and a white T-shirt and old canvas sneakers. You'd have never known I actually changed my outfit five or six times, trying to establish just the right balance of faded, chore-friendly fashion with a unique and feminine flair. I ultimately gave up and chose something to hide beneath. (The last time I wore a bathing suit, at the end of the summer, my mother grabbed me by the shoulders and exclaimed that I had an adorable little body—that I in fact looked like a sleek young harbor seal. A. Harbor. Seal. You can see why I opted for overalls.)

The work party was being held in the annex, which was what they called the big utility area connected to the back of the stage by a big set of double doors. The party was being run not by Mr. Romeo, but by Lou, who, when he was not coaching boys' soccer, designed and built sets for school productions. He looked like a no-nonsense, experienced carpenter with his worn clothes and large belly that hung over his belt like a muffin top.

I wasn't late, but there was already a flurry of activity going on. People were hammering and lifting and using screwdrivers like they'd been doing it all their lives. Scooter Nemo was actually sawing something, which made an impressive noise and left him coated with a layer of sawdust.

I immediately felt ridiculous standing there alone and useless. No one had come up to me, and everyone looked like they were in the middle of something important and shouldn't be interrupted. I tried putting my hands on my hips and frowning a little, so it would look like I was just giving some serious thought to what I should be doing.

I don't know about regular people, but I always assume people are looking at me. Closely. Just, like, as a matter of course. Wondering what I'm doing, and how I'm doing it, and why I'm doing it. I hated being here without Harper, because I couldn't look casual by talking to her. Oh, the hands on the hips thing was stupid! I changed to arms folded over my chest. Moronic! I decided on a quick trip to the bathroom.

Bathrooms, in addition to the obvious service they provide, are a wonderful sanctuary from the world. I have examined many bathrooms in my life—in restaurants, at birthday parties, sporting events. A bathroom is the perfect place to go when you have nowhere else to be, and you don't want to be where you are. No one ever sees someone going into a bathroom and wonders what they're doing. Because, you know. It's obvious.

The problem with the bathroom sanctuary is that you can only use it once per uncomfortable episode. If it's a good one, like the totally unused staff/handicapped bathroom outside the cafeteria, you could just stay inside a while, and no one would be the wiser. But there were tons of people here in the annex, and I couldn't just keep running into the bathroom every twenty minutes, particularly given my history as a nervous barfer. By the same token, once you've gone into hiding in a bathroom, the clock is ticking. You have to assume that people saw you go into the bathroom. And if you haven't come out after maybe four minutes, five maximum, they'll start to, you know. *Wonder.*

So I got safely into the bathroom, and that was a relief, but the countdown had begun. I examined the sinks, and made sure there was soap in all the dispensers. Then, just to sort of do what I ought to be doing, I actually went into a stall and locked it. But I didn't have to go, so I just stood there, making sure my feet were pointing in the correct direction. So if anyone came in, everything would look normal. I checked my watch. Stood there. Checked my watch again.

Time flies when you're hiding out in the local plumbing facilities.

There was nothing for it. I had to go back out and face them before someone came in after me. I opened the door of the stall and came out. I went to the sink and ran a little water, because I was supposed to need to wash my hands. Then I got ready to open the outer door, and I got that fluttery feeling in my stomach again.

Breathe.

Maybe I didn't have to go back out just yet. Surely another 90 seconds or so would go unnoticed? I was starting to feel relieved that I could stay in hiding a little longer when the door flew open, and the Blond Cherubic Newbie flounced in.

"Hey!" the BCN said, her face brightening when she saw me.

For an instant, I felt relief. Someone I knew! I mean, not someone that I really knew, but someone who knew me. A person I could attach myself to. So I wouldn't have to leave the bathroom alone.

"Phoebe, right? I'm Savannah! So, hey, we're both Mission Choir members! Did you learn the lines to those songs yet? What work group are you in? Isn't this whole thing a blast?"

My relief faded. I can't explain why I continued to dislike Savannah, but I did. She was so perky and cute—like a happy little chipmunk. It was embarrassing—the way she didn't try to hide her eagerness to make friends. I know it's shallow, but what would it say about me if I hung out with Savannah? Would the older Drama Club kids think I was a chipmunk too? I wasn't a chipmunk.

I gave her a half smile that pointedly did not extend to my eyes—the old "My lips are smiling but my eyes aren't" message. And I gave her a little wave that indicated I was in a hurry, with the subliminal message that I. Can't. Hang. With. You. I tried not to make it look deliberately mean, but I also had to make myself clear. There was no way I was going to join the chipmunk patrol, not with half the Drama Club just outside the door.

I burst out of the bathroom like I had somewhere to be immediately. There must be somebody I could go up to. Somebody not intimidating. What about Romalla? She had come across as shy, and therefore approachable. She had been standing off to the side by herself when I saw her before. I looked around anxiously, then spotted her next to Lou, who was offering her a choice of several different-sized hammers.

I was on my own, no way out of it. Because it would have looked stupid for me to just remain standing outside the bathroom, I marched over to a pile of something, and picked one up.

It was about the size of a bagel, with a loop that my hand slipped through. It reminded me of a loofah, but maybe one for a person with a really bad complexion. What was I supposed to do with this thing? I was starting to question my decision not to staple myself to Savannah when I had the chance. I looked around, trying not to show panic in my face. Somewhere, someone must be using one of these things.

There couldn't have been a pile of them there for no reason.

"Are you sanding?"

My heart began pounding before I even turned around. Because I knew that voice. It was the OOMA, and he had just asked me a question. *Me.*

I turned around too fast, and my voice came out with a little tremor in it.

"Am I standing? I don't . . ."

Tucker laughed. His laugh was so nice! So friendly! His dark eyes crinkled, and his hair was standing up in a way that looked unintended—like he'd just taken off a hat. I had an urge to reach up and smooth it into place. He was wearing a faded World Wildlife Fund T-shirt. His forearms were tan and muscled. He smelled like wood and paint. Yes, I was in love.

"No, are you *sanding*? You're holding a sander."

No response available. I just nodded at him. Anything I might say would probably be wrong. I couldn't risk ending my first actual two-sided conversation measuring more than five words with the OOMA by saying the wrong thing. This moment had to keep on going forever. I started to smile, but I tried to do a teeth-covered smile and my lips went funny, like I was trying to stifle a burp.

"Do you want me to help you?"

I nodded again. I could tell my face had gone

red. I was thankful to be holding the loofah-thing, because at least I had something to hold and my hands weren't flopping around uselessly.

"Follow me," said Tucker. He walked over to the wall where stacks of lumber were piled, and I had to trot like a puppy to keep up with him. I looked over my shoulder to see if Savannah the BCN, or anyone else for that matter, saw me and Tucker together. That's the thing—when you *want* people to be looking at you, it seems like they never are.

Tucker stopped at the boards, pulled one out of the pile, and stood it up next to him.

"Here we go," he said. "All the boards in this pile need to be sanded. Here, let me show you."

He reached out his hand for my loofah-thing, which I now understood to be a sander. When he took it, part of his hand touched my finger, and I had to fight to neither jerk my hand away nor grab him. He held the board in one hand and began rubbing the sander against the wood so that a fine layer of sawdust came off.

"Just rub the sander in long strokes up and down a few times, then feel the wood with your hand. It just takes a minute or so to get it smooth. You don't want to oversand it. Just make sure you get every surface of the board. When the whole thing is smooth, put it over here, and grab another one."

He held the sander out, but waited for me to ask questions. Thousands of possible questions entered my mind, detailed, difficult questions. Anything to keep him standing there for just a few more seconds. But maybe it would be cooler to just act like I knew exactly how to use a sander and that I had of course smoothed countless boards in my career both on and behind the stage, and that this was just another day for me.

"Thanks," I said. "You really know what you're doing."

You really know what you're doing? Ew, I sounded like the vice president of his preteen fan club.

He grinned.

"Yeah, I love this stuff. This actually is the main reason I'm in the Drama Club. To tell you the truth, I'm actually supposed to be in detention right now, because I forgot to show up for my math tutoring session, but there's no way I'd blow off a work party. Playing Liver Lips Louie will be fun, but what I'm really into is building sets. I think it'd be really cool to design one sometime."

"I'm sure you would be totally great!" I squeaked.

Pre. Teen. Fan. Club. Vice president.

"Listen, thanks for coming out today. Between you and me, a lot of the actress types feel like they don't have to contribute to these work parties. But if there's no set, there's no play, right? So when someone like you shows up to help, people, you know. Appreciate it. I appreciate it."

Wait. Was there some kind of *meaning* Tucker was trying to get across here? Was he just being nice, or had he kind of stressed the part about *him* appreciating me? I was going to swoon. I was going to sway dramatically, turn white as a sheet, and fall unconscious to the floor. Unless the OOMA caught me, which would be soooooo . . . romantic. . . .

". . . all morning," Tucker was saying. "So back to the staple gun for me. But let me know if you need any help."

Oh. He wasn't going to catch me. Kind of a disappointment.

"Thanks," I said. Or tried to say. It came out so soft I don't think he heard as he walked off.

I stood holding up a board, which I pretended to examine for knots so I could actually watch Tucker walk away. He went to a corner where they kept some of the major carpentry things—like electric drills and circular saws. The Experienced People's Corner. Tyler Luddo and Chris Seligman were already there, stapling large bolts of fabric to a half-built wooden structure. Chris glanced up at me for a second. Sensitive actor types sometimes can feel when someone is looking their way. I ducked my head, and started immediately and energetically sanding the wood.

It took a few minutes for me to get the feel of it. Then I actually started enjoying myself. Because it was done mostly by touch, I was able to watch the activity in the room while I sanded. There were lots more guys than girls in the annex. Both older guys, and boys I knew from my own grade. But what Tucker said was true—almost none of the girls who had parts in *Guys and Dolls* were there. There were guy actors there working, but not girls. I didn't see Delilah, or Miranda, or Mia Kezdekian. Fedora Kravitz and Annabelle Peterson were also both missing. Other than me and the BCN, only Romalla Lee Um had shown up.

The more I sanded, the more I loved it. This was perfect! I appeared busy, energetically hard at work, and yet I could observe what was going on around me. I looked like I belonged. There were at least six boards left in the pile, so I was set for probably a good twenty minutes—maybe even a half hour if I budgeted my time. I couldn't wait to call Harper and tell her that I'd successfully soloed the work party. Until I remembered that I couldn't call Harper, because we weren't speaking.

So I distracted myself by worrying about Tucker missing detention, after missing math tutoring. The OOMA seemed to show up late, or not at all, for a number of things. What if he got suspended? Expelled? What if his parents sent him away to military school to teach him discipline? I glanced discreetly in Tucker's direction, and was dismayed to see him standing next to Romalla, pointing to the hammer in her hand and saying something while she nodded energetically. I frowned. I wanted to be the only person Tucker helped during the work party. I was imagining what it would feel like to whack Romalla over the head with her own hammer when Tucker suddenly looked up at me. He gave me a quick smile, then rolled his eyes slightly. Like he had better things to do than explain hammering to Romalla. My heart leaped, and I started sanding again twice as fast as before. Had I interpreted the eye-rolling correctly? Or was it meant to be mocking me? Or did Tucker just have something in his eye?

"Hey again!"

Savannah was standing in front of me, looking a little flustered as she tucked a blond tendril behind one ear.

"Hey," I said, then moved the sander hard and fast over the wood so she could see how busy I was.

Savannah leaned in toward me, and I had to stop sanding or the dust would have gotten in her hair.

"Phoebe, I'm kind of not sure what to do. Everybody seems so busy already. Is there any way I can help you do what you're doing?"

I scowled. I was the sander! Me! It wasn't fair that now the BCN also wanted to be a sander. I had found the perfect job, and now she wanted to muscle in on my territory. But I could see the anxiety in her eyes, and I knew precisely what she was feeling. I had been feeling the same thing just minutes ago. Reluctantly, I picked up another sander and handed it to her.

"There's nothing to it," I said. "Just run the sander over every surface of the board until it's all smooth. But don't oversand. The pile of boards that need work is right there."

Savannah took the sander as if I were handing her the world's largest ruby.

"Oh Phoebe, *thank* you! I was starting to think I was going to have to stand around like an idiot all afternoon!"

"It's fine," I said. It wasn't fine, actually. It was irritating as all get out. But I felt guilty about being unfriendly to Savannah when her only crime was being a happy chipmunk. Maybe I had made up for it a little now, but I still felt kind of bad.

"Isn't this fun? Can you believe this is all going to be assembled into a set by the end of the week? It's incredible what Lou can do, totally incredible."

Her chattering soon washed away my guilt and

replaced it with more irritation. I nodded grimly.

"I just hope there are enough people here," Savannah continued. "It seems like all the guys turned out, except for Ben and Bud. And the two girls I know are both from soccer. I don't think they're even on the regular crew. Not to be catty or anything, but doesn't it seem like we're the only actresses here except for Romalla?"

I did not want to have a talky, chipmunky conversation with Savannah. But we *were* the only actresses there besides Romalla, and I *did* find it kind of annoying, especially in light of what Tucker had said. Actresses not showing up to a work call was a personal insult to Tucker.

"Yeah, I know. I mean, this isn't required or anything, but it seems like the people who are actually going to be *on* the stage should be the first ones to pitch in."

"Exactly!" said Savannah, her face brightening. She leaned closer to me.

"I've heard," she whispered, "that some of the girls who get cast a lot sort of have . . . attitudes. About the backstage work and stuff. That they feel kind of, you know. Above it."

I was torn between getting into a full-on dish session with Savannah, and remaining aloof and superior. Plus, there were my new friendships to protect.

"I don't know," I said, my eyes on my board. "Delilah seems really cool. She dropped by my house last week, you know. Just as a friendly thing. And Mia Kezdekian has been pretty nice to me."

I peeked at Savannah to see if my name-dropping was impressing her. I'm sure she never realized I was kind of in with the older crowd.

"Well, all I know is what I heard. People say Delilah can be a real back-stabber. And I've heard she and Mia hate each other. But I don't know Mia at all. She's never really talked to me, to be honest."

I felt a little smug satisfaction that Savannah admitted Mia had never spoken to her. And she obviously didn't know Delilah well either. I mean, plainly there was no knife sticking out of my back. I sanded silently for the next few minutes, trying to look totally and utterly absorbed in my craftsmanship.

"Wow, that was the last one," I heard Savannah say.

I looked up and couldn't believe it. We'd sanded every board in the pile. Thanks to Savannah, I was once again unemployed.

"I guess I could go ask Lou if he needs painters yet," Savannah said. "Do you want to go with me?"

I did, actually. Because otherwise I was going

to end up standing alone once again, with all my boards sanded and no prospects. But I caught sight of the OOMA across the room just as he was looking over. He pointed to the pile of finished boards and gave me the thumbs-up. Maybe he was going to come back over!

"No thanks, Savannah. I'm just going to check a few pieces over. Make sure I didn't miss anything."

"Oh, okay." Savannah sounded genuinely disappointed, and I started feeling guilty again. But she had already started in Lou's direction.

"See you later, Phee!"

I gave her a little wave, a frown on my face. I *hated* it when people I didn't know shortened my name, especially when they shortened it to the wrong thing. Was I calling her Sav or Nah all of a sudden? One mutual sanding session did not make us Best Friends Forever. Anyway, my nickname had a *b* and an *s* on the end. Pheebs, plural. At least Tucker hadn't come over while the BCN was glued to my side. I couldn't wait to tell Harper about how Tucker had helped me, and about the eye-rolling thing. Then I remembered all over again. Why did I keep forgetting, and thinking things were happy and normal? Why weren't they? Would they ever be again, or was this my life now?

"Hey, all done! You're fast!"

I had been so absorbed in brooding over Harper, I hadn't even seen Tucker coming over. I felt a little more confident now, still holding my sander, so I looked up at him and smiled a full-teeth smile.

"Thanks," I said. "I like sanding."

Finally! I had produced both a regular smile and a short sentence!

"You did a great job," he said. "Like a pro."

"Oh, I'm not a pro," I said. "But I liked it. Something about the way the wood feels as it gets smoother, and the way it smells—I don't know, it just—it's really relaxing. Like the wood and I were in sync . . . Or something."

Was I INSANE? Where was this philosophical meditation on wood coming from? I mean yes, I *had* felt that way, but saying it to Tucker made me sound like—like a CRAZY person!

Except that Tucker wasn't looking at me like I was crazy.

"Oh man, that's like, exactly it!" he said, smiling. "I mean, I love working with wood but I've never really been able to put the reason into words, and you just totally nailed it! No pun intended. But seriously, that's so cool."

Okay. Maybe not SO insane.

I searched for more conversation about the Zen of Woodworking, but came up short.

"Well, like I said, thanks for showing up today," Tucker said.

I beamed from ear to ear.

"I think you and Savannah are like the only new girls that came."

My smile faded a little. Why did he have to lump me in with *her*?

"If you don't have to go yet, Lou could probably use you to do some painting."

I ordered the smile to return to my face.

"Definitely. I'd definitely like to help paint. Definitely!"

Losers repeat words three times. Losers. Losers!

But Tucker was giving me such a gorgeous smile, it was like the sun had just risen inside the annex.

"Thanks, Pheebs. You're the best. Let me know if you need help with anything."

He had called me Pheebs! I could barely breathe through the happiness.

The OOMA was already halfway back to his staple-gun corner. I stood just a moment more, letting it all sink in.

It killed me to admit it, but Harper *had* been right about one thing yesterday.

I *definitely* wanted to play Spin the Bottle.

CHAPTER NINE
T-Minus Three Weeks

My mother does this irritating thing on the first Thursday of every month. Actually, my mother does many irritating things. But this particular one is actually written on the calendar.

She calls it Talk Yoga. People uniting their voices and feelings to stretch and explore new levels of emotional flexibility. That's how she explains it, anyway. What it means to me is that on the first Thursday each month, meaning today, ten anxious, confused, and angry people show up at our house to seek emotional well-being by babbling and shouting like a bunch of civilly disobedient chickens.

To be honest, it wasn't in and of itself such a bad thing. It actually showed a really nice side of my mother—because Talk Yoga was something she did for free, for people who couldn't afford to go to therapy but needed a little help expressing their feelings. For all her therapy-talk and feel-good stuff, deep down my mother was the real thing. When she said stuff like "Plant love in your backyard and that's what will grow all over your world," it's because she actually believed it. She wasn't a shrink for the power, or the money. She was just one of those people who, you know, always want to help. Like a fireman, but for feelings.

But while I appreciated the kindness of Talk Yoga, personally it was a little distracting. Sometimes I managed to be out of the house during the session, but since Talk Yoga was on a school night, that wasn't always possible. On nights I couldn't flee, I barricaded myself in my room and experimented with how loud I could get my iPod to play without making my teeth ache.

But I couldn't hide between earbuds this particular Thursday evening. Because after four days of rehearsals that focused solely on any scene except one in which I had something to do, tomorrow I was up for both a sing-rehearsal and a blocking rehearsal. Though it sounds more like something you'd practice in football, blocking is in fact the process by which the director and the actor agree where and how the actor will move and speak in a scene. I had only two spoken lines in the entire play, and they were both in the scene we would be rehearsing. There was also a rumor that each of the Mission Choir members was going to be assigned a bit of business to do during one of the singing scenes. The fact that Harper would be there made me even more tense.

So Friday's rehearsal was going to be a big day for me. And though I had only two lines, I took them very seriously. I had highlighted them with a yellow pen in the script, just as Chris Seligman had highlighted his pages and pages of speeches. I had memorized both my lines to a fault, and declaimed them loudly every morning in the shower.

I was now determined to spend some very serious time with my script establishing a backstory for my character within the *Guys and Dolls* story line. Why was my character in the Salvation Army? What did she think? What did I *as* the character think of my boss, Sergeant Sarah? What did I want, and what had I left behind? Shampoo with or without conditioner? Toast or cereal for breakfast?

These were all questions that a serious actress, even one with only a few lines, should be putting thought into before an important rehearsal. And that was a little difficult now that Talk Yoga was in full session, and at least two of my mother's clients seemed to be flexing their emotional connections with operatic gusto.

Maybe my character had joined the Salvation Army and left the material world behind because she had found her soul mate, but she had barfed in front of him, so he never asked her out. Maybe she had a big fight with her best friend and never fully recovered. Maybe my character was trapped by her Outer Self, and finally gave up trying to be seen and retreated into the world of charitable service.

I curled up in my beanbag chair with my script in front of me, a tall glass of Ovaltine, some crackers, and an orange nearby (I had learned to stock up provisions ahead of time to avoid going downstairs during Talk Yoga). I tried to tune out everything but the Mission Choir and my own character, who I had decided to name Hortensia Godfrey since she was designated only as "Mission Choir Member #3" in the script.

Unfortunately, a Yoga Talker downstairs with a particularly deep baritone voice began exploring his psyche by shouting something about wanting a play-date with his inner child over and over again. The noise seemed to be rising straight through the living room ceiling and funneling directly into the center of my beanbag chair.

"This is ridiculous!" I exclaimed, slapping the

script against my legs for dramatic emphasis. I stretched Tonky Butt over my head like a misshapen pair of ear-muffs, but the sound came through loud and clear.

Normally at a point like this I would call Harper. And it seemed the longer I *didn't* call Harper, the more determined I became to *keep* not calling her. Also, it was starting to really wig me out that Harper had not called *me*. She was the one who had dismissed everything I was interested in. She was the one who had criticized me, lectured me. How could she not realize by now that she was the one who needed to reach out? What was going on? Had Harper been secretly wanting to get rid of me and jumped at this opportunity?

It was unthinkable that Harper and I would not be best friends. Nobody else made me feel so content in my own skin, so completely seen. Nobody else begged for me to do my impressions, then cried for laughing so hard. I was never going to meet anyone as gifted and loyal as Harper Tanaka. No one would ever trust me with their secrets, or be able to create the world's next great comic strip with me. And I knew, because we'd talked about it, that Harper felt the same way about me. Unless she had changed her mind.

Before I even realized I'd started crying, my face

was covered with tears. I was doing that deep gasping thing between sobs. Before today, I had never actually thought Harper and I might be through forever. That thought made nothing seem more important than Harper. Not Delilah, or Mia. Not even the OOMA. I just wanted things to be the way they used to be.

My mother always says that if you want to cry, you should let it go full force. Then, at some moment you'll feel is the right time, you should tell yourself that it's enough, and that you are taking control of yourself again. Actually, what she suggests is saying out loud "My emotions are not the boss of me," but I find that kind of embarrassing. The basic idea behind it, though, isn't bad. Because otherwise a person could either hold in their emotions and become a robot, or they could sit around crying all day. All week. Maybe even all year, if things were bad enough. And that would certainly take its toll on a girl's complexion. So I took a deep breath and told myself (silently) that I'd had my cry and it had been a good one, and that it was over now.

As I wiped the wet stuff off my face with Tonky Butt's tail, I looked around the room for something within reach of my beanbag to distract me. I saw one of my movie magazines lying where I'd left it, only half read. I dropped my script onto the floor and put the magazine on my lap in its place, flipping through the glossy pages in search of an article that would blot out the possible permanent loss of Harper from my consciousness.

A headline caught my attention.

Kattra Samson—Her Amazing Transformation from an Anonymous Wallflower to Hollywood's Hottest Young Star!

I examined Kattra's full-page color photograph. Her nose had a bit of a bump in it, and her lips curved down, giving her expression a hint of meanness. Still, she was a stunner, no doubt about it. The piece was followed by a rundown of what beauty products I might consider purchasing if I wanted to achieve Kattra's look.

I examined the picture again.

I didn't need to look in the mirror to know that no amount of Clarins Hydra-Matte Day Lotion and Eye Contour Balm was going to make the Outer Me look like Kattra Samson. I knew that my lips would never be pouty and hint at meanness. I would not look edgy with a bump on the bridge of my nose—I would look like a klutz who had walked into a wall.

I was no Kattra Samson. Kattra Samson had no bearing on my life whatsoever. It was Phoebe Hart that I needed to worry about. I reached over and grabbed the orange. I held it in front of my face and examined it. I gave it a small, mysterious smile. I half blinked my eyelids lazily, while gazing at the fruit with piercing intensity. Then I pursed my lips. The orange, clearly sharing my romantic intent, moved closer. A second later, we were kissing. As I kept my eyes closed, I tried to really *feel* the moment, to *be* the moment, like we did in scene exercises at Young Protégé Acting Camp. This was no regular orange, it was the OOMA of oranges, and I . . . I was Kattra Samson—tall, slightly threatening, and confident. I felt . . . stupid. I threw the orange down, or maybe it fled, dismayed by our obvious lack of chemistry.

More than ever, I knew I had to put everything into my acting. I was not remarkable-looking and I was not a naturally talented kisser, but with commitment, I might one day learn to act like I was.

Mr. Romeo wanted all the Mission Choir members onstage along with Delilah Fortescue. We were going to rehearse our first scene together—after marching through the sin-filled streets of New York with our small band (trumpet, triangle, and drum) singing "Follow the Fold," we stop outside our headquarters, the Save-A-Soul Mission, where Sergeant Sarah Brown is about to meet the dashing Sky Masterson for the first time.

I was extremely thankful to be onstage and at attention—it was one of the few activities that could temporarily take my mind off Harper. She was sitting at the little director's table that Mr. Romeo had set up in the auditorium, along with Miss Maslin and Scooter Nemo, who was the stage manager. She hadn't looked up when I arrived, but just the sight of her studiously writing with her shiny brown hair tucked behind one ear and a roll of peppermint Life Savers near her clipboard brought a huge lump to my throat. But I could not cry. Must not. This was acting—the one thing in my life that could take me out of myself and make me something different, no matter what. So I swallowed the lump and joined the others onstage.

We'd gone over the hymn with Miss Maslin and all of us had memorized the entire thing. Now Mr. Romeo was teaching us to march in character and sing at the same time. It's more complicated than it sounds. We had to start singing offstage, then enter mid-song, and keep singing until we reached the mission door, then sing the last line of the hymn there on the sidewalk. Then we had to file into the mission to put our stuff away, and be in the background looking surprised and curious when Sky walked in. As Mr. Romeo explained, it was crucial that we not sing too fast. Or walk too fast. Otherwise we'd run out of hymn before arriving at the mission, or we'd have too much hymn left over before going through the door. Mr. Romeo had us practice it four times until we finally got it close to right.

If I hadn't been masking my underlying misery and pretending not to notice Harper, I'd say the rehearsal was the most fun I'd had in months. Seriously. I was finally one of "them"—the kids on the real stage with actual lights doing a proper show. I could have gone over my scene for hours without getting tired of it. I just wish I had been able to enjoy it a little more.

Delilah's scene when Sergeant Sarah meets Sky was scheduled to rehearse that afternoon, but since Delilah was actually in our scene too, her presence was required during our blocking. I guess she was trying to save her strength, because for part of the rehearsal she sat in the second row with her feet propped up and a pair of white sunglasses with lenses the size of saucers over her eyes. Once we'd gotten our timing right, though, Mr. Romeo told her she needed to be up onstage with us.

When we ran the scene for the last time our timing went a bit off, and we stood around discussing which of us was jumping the gun, and who was lagging behind. Delilah stood off to one side, her hands on her hips, tapping one foot like she was trying to communicate through Morse code. When Mr. Romeo went over to the director's table to have a quiet discussion with Miss Maslin, Delilah made a noise through her nose that communicated a high level of irritation.

"The chorus needs to have this stuff worked out *before* I come onstage to rehearse with you," she hissed in our direction. "This is all you guys have to do. I have an entire *play* to work on. I'm the *lead*. I can't waste time standing here while you try to figure out how to do the one stupid thing you have to do."

Then she turned on her heel and strode offstage, past the big garbage can whose interior I had once unhappily inspected. I looked over at Mr. Romeo to see if he had heard this, but he seemed fully absorbed in his whispered discussion with Miss Maslin. Then I gave a quick glance in Harper's direction with my eyelids half lowered and my head turned to the side, so it wouldn't look like I was looking. She was sketching something on a piece of paper. I wondered if it was a character for "My Not So Alien Life." Would Harper keep working on the strip now that we weren't doing it together?

"What's her problem?" Savannah whispered. "This is our first time rehearsing this scene on the stage— she's been up here for a week getting used to it!"

I shrugged, because I wasn't sure how far Delilah had walked and I didn't want to say anything she might overhear.

Our sole male Mission Choir member, a round pleasant-faced eighth grader named Andrew, sidled over when he heard Savannah whispering.

"Notice she said that loud enough for us to hear, but not loud enough for Mr. Romeo," Andrew murmured, his eyes narrowing royally. "She butters him up and he buys it. Then she turns into this nightmare diva when his back is turned."

Dana, the final member of our chorus, stood off to one side with her hands clasped in front of her and her eyes gazing downward. She looked like a mortician.

"She's not interested in this scene because she doesn't have any lines in it. We're singing, so the audience is actually looking at *us*. And she doesn't like it," Savannah said.

Andrew nodded, while I tried to look like I neither agreed nor disagreed. I was secretly stung by Delilah's criticism of the chorus. Because when she put things that way, we did seem like the amateur losers of the production.

Mr. Romeo was still conferring with Miss Maslin, when he glanced up and seemed to notice us standing there for the first time.

"People, why don't we go ahead and take a ten-minute break here," he half called, half sang.

Andrew and Savannah drifted off toward the seats,

casting glances at me like they were expecting me to drift with them. But I turned and walked backstage in the direction Delilah had gone.

I saw her almost immediately, standing by the doors to the annex talking to Bud. At first I started to duck out of sight, but then I decided to just walk over. After all, Delilah had come to my house as a gesture of friendship. Surely it was okay to go over to her and start a conversation. After I'd decided to do it, though, I started to get nervous. This was Delilah, after all. And I was only a seventh grader, and running the usual risk that the Outer Me would sabotage the Inner Me. But you have to try, I told myself. With the way things are going with Harper you might not have any friends right now. Just do it.

So I did. I walked straight over to where Delilah was standing. She was speaking intently to Bud, and didn't see me coming.

" . . . trying to tolerate these chorus morons!" she was saying. "I can't deal with you pulling stuff like this on top of that! Don't you realize how it would look? How it would reflect on me? You and I weren't going out yet last time, but we are now. You're not playing, Bud, and that's all there is to it."

"Get over yourself," Bud said. "You are so lame this year—you sound like an old married lady. If I want to play, I'm playing."

Then he caught sight of me. Delilah was still completely focused on Bud, and she was breathing in little pre-crying gasps.

"Can you please just—"

"Later," Bud said, making a beeline for the backstage exit.

Delilah looked stunned to find herself standing there alone. She started rubbing at her eyes, and I wondered how to turn and walk away without making it obvious that I'd overheard the last part of their exchange. Leave it to me to get the courage to approach Delilah at the exact wrong time. I didn't know what was going on, but I did know Bud wasn't being very nice to his girlfriend.

That's when she looked up and noticed me standing there. Was she going to be mad that I'd seen her like this? Her mouth went into a little O of surprise, then she rearranged her face into a smile.

"Phoebe. Ick, I'm like, having this major allergy attack—I'm like, miserable!"

Okay. If Delilah wanted to play the allergy card, that was fine with me.

"Yeah, I know the feeling," I said. "I get hay fever in the spring, and I walk around for weeks with a big red nose and watery eyes."

Which I immediately regretted saying, because it

Taking Stars test

implied that Delilah had a big red nose and watery eyes. Which she kind of did.

"Luckily it looks like you don't get it as bad as I do," I added quickly, and yeah, lamely. But Delilah smiled and nodded.

"No, I know," she said. "It just gives me a head-ache, you know, and it makes me more irritable when rehearsal is going slowly. Which is why it's so great that *you* are in the Mission Choir, Phoebe, because you are so professional. You're the backbone of the chorus, and you should definitely know that. It's so obvious that you've studied! You know, not just this part, but studied your *craft*."

I flushed with pleasure at the compliment. Because I *had* studied, excessively. I was probably the only Mission Choir member who had actually named her character. I knew what Hortensia Godfrey had con-sumed for breakfast (dry unbuttered toast and weak tea). And my Young Protégé Acting Camp training was clearly standing me in very good stead in the rehearsal process. I'm sorry if it seemed disloyal to my Mission Choir peers, but maybe Delilah was the only student qualified enough to realize that my work was on a different level than the other newbies'.

"Oh, I have," I said. "I've worked up a backstory for my character. I totally know all the hymns and both my lines."

Delilah was nodding, which for some reason I took as encouragement and approval, so I kept talking.

"Actually, Delilah, I mean it's a secret and everything, but with all the trouble that Miranda's been having with her voice . . . I kind of went ahead and learned her lines and blocking. You know, in case they should suddenly need someone at the last minute."

Delilah gave me an unreadable, bug-eyed look. Had I over-shared?

"I mean, it's stupid, actually. It's not like I think . . . I'm not trying to climb over anyone or anything. It's just that when Mia told me what was going on with Miranda's voice, she sort of suggested I learn the part, as—"

"Mia Kezdekian told you to learn Miranda's part?" Delilah asked sharply.

Whoops. Over-share number two.

"Oh, no, I mean, you know. Not exactly. We were just chatting one day, about things and stuff, and the show came up of course, so we were just . . . and then she said something about being worried Miranda might have to drop out, and that if someone learned—that if I were to—"

I was just making it worse, having it come out sounding like some kind of plot when it wasn't. Delilah's lips had gone into a tight little line. There was only one possible way out of this—an abrupt subject change.

"Hey, I just remembered I have a chewable Benadryl in my bookbag which is great for allergies! Do you want me to run and get it for you?"

Delilah put one finger in the air, near her ear. Accomplished actress that she was, it was clear to me that she meant "Shhh—I'm listening to something."

"Mr. Romeo's calling me. He must have some notes for me," she said.

I hadn't heard anything, but Delilah was already walking back toward the scrim curtain to the stage. I stood there alone, almost groaning aloud. I had definitely done something wrong, but I wasn't sure what. Was it because I thought I was good enough to step into Miranda Goetz's shoes? Was it because I'd just blundered on Delilah arguing with her boyfriend? Or maybe it was because, in my eagerness to impress her, I'd momentarily forgotten Delilah and Mia hated each other.

Oops.

Well, I wasn't going to be able to fix it at that moment. I'd have to think about it, bide my time, and watch how things played out. I was still standing there thinking when I heard someone come up the stairs that led to the backstage area from the prop room and costume shop. It was Tucker, looking out of breath and slightly more rumpled than usual. He was holding a Mountain Dew soda in each hand. He stopped when he saw me. Actually, he did a kind of double take. Oh no—was my proximity to the Barf Can causing him to remember my shame?

"Oh. Pheebs. I didn't—I wasn't—I am so busted."

"You're what?" I asked.

"Um . . . Has Mr. Romeo noticed I wasn't here?"

"Oh. I don't think so. I mean, I haven't heard him asking for you. He hasn't given the call for the next scene. Not yet."

Tucker gave a relieved sigh.

"I totally spaced that rehearsal was starting—I mean, don't think I'm a total idiot or anything. I'm not always—It's just that the vending machine by the gym broke and was giving away free sodas, and I thought— What scene are we doing? Am I supposed to be here now?"

His face was totally red.

"Well, we just finished the first Mission Choir scene, and they're supposed to do the one with Sarah and Sky. And we're also doing the one where Nathan Detroit and the guys are trying to figure out where they can go and play dice."

"That's the one I'm in!" Tucker said. "Okay, cool. Seriously, I'm not always . . . I can actually be kind of . . ."

He stopped talking and handed me a Mountain Dew, which I took. His face was still red. Had something bad just happened that he didn't want to talk about? The OOMA was acting very weird. And did he just want me to hold the soda, or was it kind of like . . . a present?

Tucker cleared his throat, and looked around.

"So listen, Pheebs."

I did.

"I . . . Not that you necessarily . . . Sorry. Pheebs."

I clutched the soda like it was the Holy Grail and he was Lancelot.

"Sorry," he repeated. "I just—I have to ask you a question."

It was then that the unmistakable sound of Mr. Romeo calling for the next scene actors to be onstage assaulted my ears.

"Oh. I better . . ."

"It might be your scene," I said helpfully.

"Thanks," Tucker said. Then he hightailed it out of there.

What. Had. Just. Happened?

Calm down, I told myself. It was nothing. Nothing happened. The OOMA was late, and gave me a

soda. A Mountain Dew is not the carbonated equiv-
alent of a diamond ring.

But what was the OOMA trying to ask? He'd been
about to say it.

Oh—thwarted by Mr. Romeo!

I stared at the soda for a moment. In the crimson
light of the fire exit sign, its silvery glistening shape
looked like the most beautiful thing in the world.
Either something, or nothing, had just happened.
I needed help. I needed to analyze everything the
OOMA had said, everything he hadn't said, everything he might have said. I needed Harper.

Onstage I could hear voices. The actors were about
to start running the scene. What was I supposed to
do now? Saunter out like nothing had happened? But
nothing *had* happened, I reminded myself. Right? I
peeked around the curtain, and saw that they were
actually about to do Delilah's scene, the one before
Tucker's. They hadn't started yet, so I walked across
the stage toward the seats, where Savannah and
Andrew were sitting cross-legged on the stairs by the
front row, talking intently. I kept my eyes on them, so
that I could clearly be NOT looking at or for Tucker.
Savannah and Andrew looked up when they saw me.

"Phee, where did you go? We wanted to get your
opinion on something! Come sit down—we only
have like four minutes left of break."

I was torn. I wanted to go sit with them. The BCN was so irritatingly consistent in her attempt to make friends with me that I was actually starting to warm up to her a tiny, tiny bit, even if she did say my nickname wrong.

But I had zillions of thoughts assaulting my brain. I needed to memorize every aspect of the exchange with Tucker while it was still fresh in my mind. That meant now. I was also still freaked about the thing with Delilah. How was it going to look to her if I immediately went back and hung out with Savannah and Andrew, no doubt to gossip about everything, including Delilah's diva attitude? Or to the OOMA—might he think I was talking about *him*? For that matter, how would it look to Harper? She might think I'd moved on already, palling around with the BCN. And if she thought I'd moved on, she might never come back to me.

So instead I shrugged and waved at Savannah and Andrew, then pointed at the seats to indicate there was something important in that direction that I needed to do. Savannah looked a little hurt, but then Andrew tapped her on the knee and started talking again, and soon Savannah's wide, chipmunk grin had reappeared.

I went and sat out the rest of the Mission Choir's break in a seat near the front row, on the opposite side of the theater from the director's table. I could see part of the side of Harper's face from where I was sitting, but I was pretty sure I wasn't in her peripheral vision. Not that she was looking around for me. And I couldn't see Tucker from where I was sitting either. The BCN and Andrew were still chattering and I wondered what they were saying. But I didn't get up. I sat all by myself, clutching my Mountain Dew to my chest. Obsessing all alone felt stupid. And I hated that Harper knew perfectly well that I was sitting by myself with no one to talk to, and yet she did nothing about it.

The theater can be a lonely place.

CHAPTER TEN
T-Minus Ten Days

As we got progressively closer to opening night, I didn't have to worry—Harperless as I was—about what to do with my free time. Between rehearsing, work calls, homework, and sneaking time to secretly memorize Miranda's lines and blocking, I barely had two minutes to myself.

Now when I ran into Tucker in the hall, or ended up in his vicinity during rehearsal, he always talked to me. He always seemed friendly. But it was impossible to tell if he was just being regulation friendly or if he was going out of his way to talk to me. On the one hand, being friendly was just in his nature. On the other hand, he was sometimes weirdly . . . *weird* when he talked to me. But he never brought up The Question.

I had kept the Mountain Dew can. It was currently sitting on my dresser, where I could see it from bed. This morning, the Mountain Dew can was the first thing I'd seen when I opened my eyes. And Tucker was the first person I'd thought of. What if Tucker actually did like me? What if he didn't? I couldn't decide which was worse: to be heartachingly consumed with a guy and not know if he liked you, or to know for a fact that he didn't. Maybe Tucker had just picked up on my crush, and my awkwardness occasionally weirded him out. And maybe when it seemed like he was acting friendly, he was just being considerate of a poor, delusional, lovesick girl. You know. Charity niceness.

Because he *did* do nice little things for everybody. If someone spilled the contents of their bookbag, or couldn't get their locker open, or lost something, Tucker would be right there, helping out. When an eighth grader named Tillie thought she'd lost one of the pearl earrings her grandmother gave her and started crying in gym, Tucker talked to her until she felt better, and helped her search the floor until the earring was found. When Ben Pfeiffer discovered the pen in his pocket had exploded, Tucker lent him a clean T-shirt (and I was secretly relieved to discover it wasn't only girls he helped out).

He was just a nice guy, plain and simple. He was

also the most chronically disorganized person I'd ever known. Tucker always seemed to be rushing to make up assignments he'd missed, or forgetting to go somewhere he had to be, or showing up in the wrong place at the wrong time. To me, this just made him more thoroughly lovable. But since I was always exactly where I was supposed to be and never forgot my homework, it was probably all the more likely he didn't think we were soul mates.

Then there was Delilah. I'd sort of hoped we would work past the allergy moment, and there were times I thought we had. But Delilah never seemed to be the same person twice. There were times when I thought she was definitely acting mad at me, and then suddenly she'd be there at a rehearsal telling me loudly what a great job I was doing. But then I might walk up to her before a rehearsal and get totally blown off. It was bewildering and depressing. Rejected by my best friend, probably unrecognized as a soul mate by the Object of My Affection, and blown off by the star and president of the Drama Club, all in the first month of middle school.

I tried to hide it all from my mother, pretending to be suffering from theatrical exhaustion when she carefully approached me with her eyebrows scrunched with worry. I explained away Harper's absence from my social life by saying that neither of us had the time to hang out while the show was going on, which was technically true, but if we hadn't been in a fight, we would have found a way. Whenever my mother was around, I carefully produced the air of a girl who was tired and overscheduled, but not upset about anything in particular. I thought I was doing a fairly convincing job. That is, until my mother came to my room one night bearing a tall glass of Ovaltine and a Deeply Concerned Expression.

"Thirsty?" she asked, handing me the chocolate drink.

There are some things it is difficult to pretend you don't want, even if you are a good actress. Chocolate is on top of that list. I took the Ovaltine.

"Thanks," I said, taking a good long chug.

"Chocolate mustache," my mother said with a smile, reaching for my upper lip with one finger.

I beat her to the punch, wiping my lip with my sleeve—a disgusting habit left over from elementary school.

"Haven't seen much of you these past few weeks," she said, sitting on the edge of my bed.

"Yeah, Mr. Romeo warned us it would be crazy—practically no free time, and no letup on homework and stuff, so it's keeping me pretty busy. Plus, I've been learning this other girl's lines just in case they need someone to step in because she's been sick . . . Long story. Probably won't happen. But the show is only ten days away—after that I'll be back to normal again."

"Good. Are you—I mean, is it everything you hoped it would be? You've been talking about that Drama Club for so many years now. Is it what you thought it would be like? Are the kids nice?"

I didn't want to sit down right next to my mother on the bed, and the beanbag chair was too difficult to negotiate with eight ounces of Ovaltine in one hand, so I just stayed where I was, standing by the window. When I spoke my voice sounded unnaturally cheerful.

"Oh yeah, definitely. Definitely!"

My mother nodded and smiled, but I knew she was onto me. At least she was keeping the shrink talk to a minimum so far. No "And how do you feel about that" or "What do you think that means."

"I'm glad to hear that, Phoebe. I am. And it must be difficult to keep up with your schoolwork when so much of your time is going to the Drama Club. Even so . . . You haven't exactly seemed . . . yourself recently."

I raised both eyebrows and widened my eyes. My expression said: Me? Not myself? Really?

"On top of the extra work and the stress of the production, I just feel like there's something else that's eating at you, Pheebs. I'm worried."

It wasn't a lie, exactly, to simply stand there wide-eyed and blinking. So that's what I did.

"Okay honey, don't get mad at me. But I think I might know what's bothering you."

Oh, no. She must have talked to Harper's mother. They were like heads of state—they had totally different worldviews and didn't really hang out together, but from time to time they had a polite summit meeting to catch up.

"No, it isn't," I said, aware that my mother hadn't offered her theory yet, so my vague denial made no sense.

"Just hear me out for a minute," my mother said. She pulled the cloth scrunchie out of her hair, and her graying curls bounced down. She looked nicer that way, softer.

"I ran into one of the PTA moms who's organizing a workshop for Parents and Peer Pressure. We got to talking a little, and I mentioned you being in the Drama Club. She said it puts a great deal of stress on the kids, and that a lot is expected of them."

"I'm fine with that, Mom, I told you," I said.

"I know, Phoebe. But this woman also mentioned something else that she'd heard, though her child isn't in the club. Something about opening night. Apparently the kids all have to play Spin the Bottle."

I looked up, alarmed. This was the last thing I thought my mother was going to bring up, or even know about. Just to hear her saying the words Spin the Bottle and apparently understand their meaning was horrifying.

"Mom!" I said, outraged and desperate for her to drop it.

"I take it you know what the game is, then," she said.

I gave her a look of desperate discomfort.

"Well, I'm sorry honey, but we need to be able to talk frankly about this. When I heard about the game, and how everyone is pressured to play it, I realized that might very well be what's been bothering you. You've just left elementary school. You don't have any experience with boys. I mean, do you?"

I just stared at her. The horror.

"Honey, it's really not fair to kids like you. I don't expect you to completely understand the issues, but to put pressure on girls your age to play a kissing game is so inappropriate on so many levels. You know, going from sixth to seventh grade is a huge transition, socially as well as scholastically. And given that your middle school goes through ninth grade, you're suddenly rubbing shoulders with older teenagers. I have to say, I don't think having the ninth graders in with the middle school is such a good idea. You're still a kid, sweetie! No boy should be . . . You're not even equipped to . . . You're not ready to—I mean, do you think you're ready for something like that?"

Ew. Yick. Ack.

"Mom, please," I mumbled.

"Phoebe, I know I'm embarrassing you. Believe me, I know. I wouldn't be having this conversation with you unless I thought it was truly important."

"Yiflah," I stammered.

"Just hear me out for another minute," my mother urged. She patted the bed next to where she was sitting. "Come here. Come sit."

Like sitting next to her wouldn't make this even *more* excruciating. As a shrink, you'd think she'd know that. But I did what she asked. She smelled good—like her special organic shampoo and lavender. I bit the side of my mouth to help me focus and keep my cool and calm composure.

"I just want to know if you're feeling uncomfortable about this . . . game. Do the kids really push everybody to play? Even the seventh graders? Is it something you feel like you have to do in order to be accepted?"

No Mom, actually I recently encountered my soul mate when he was searching for a Frisbee on the playground and I saw his soul through the windows of his eyes, and he is kind and warm-hearted and so good-looking it makes your head spin, and I'm bound and determined to play the game because it may well be the only chance I'll ever get in my life to have him kiss me.

"I don't know," I said.

My mother sighed—a deep, long one that didn't bode well for her take on the conversation.

"Okay, let me ask you something else. How's Harper with all this?"

I swallowed. This was going from bad to worse.

"How *is* she with it?" I repeated the question.

"Well Pheebs, she's in the Drama Club too. How does she feel about the game? Harper has always struck me as someone not easily swayed by the pack. I'm sure you two have talked about it—she's your best friend. Does she feel pressured too? Does she feel something is being asked of her before she's ready for it?"

Actually Mom, Harper remains solely interested in studying, creating comic strips, investigating the outbreak of super-viruses, and brushing up on quantum physics string theory. She continues to view boys as alien life-forms. She is above being swayed by the pack. She is better than that. She is better than me.

"Phoebe, did you hear me?"

I looked over at her, because I wasn't sure if she'd asked another question that I hadn't heard.

My mother leaned over and pressed her shoulder

against mine, squeezing my wrist with one hand.

"Pheebs, honey. What about Harper?"

Well. Yeah. That was the Sixty-Thousand-Dollar Question.

What about Harper?

Before I could even think of a way to stop it, I started crying, and by the time three or four tears had streaked down my face, I was bawling at the top of my lungs.

"Oh honey," my mom said, and she pulled my head onto her lap and held me there running her fingers through my hair. And I let her.

"Cry it out," she murmured. "Cry it out good."

And she didn't ask anything else, didn't press for details or even tell me that it was all going to be fine. She just let me do what I needed to do, and all the time she rubbed my back and was just there.

Even when I finally stopped, when the emotions weren't the boss of me anymore, as she would say, there weren't any more questions. She just handed me the half-empty glass of Ovaltine, and nodded as I drank the rest down in one gulp. Then she took the glass and left my room quietly, leaving me alone to think about the only thing that was really bothering me—the only thing that had been on my mind non-stop for so long.

What *about* Harper?

CHAPTER ELEVEN
T-Minus Eight Days

It happened at rehearsal a couple of days later. We were running the final staging in the last scene, when both Sergeant Sarah and Adelaide are wearing wedding dresses, and we all know they are both going to be united in matrimonial bliss with their boyfriends.

It was one of the few scenes I was in with Mia Kezdekian. Mia's character of Adelaide and Sergeant Sarah had scenes together, but my Mission Choir was usually not around at those times. The way Mr. Romeo had decided our finale would be staged, the entire cast would squeeze onto the stage for what looked to be a double wedding. The Mission Choir had a moment when they started singing "For She's a Jolly Good Fellow." After a few lines, the rest of the cast would join in, and we would follow it up by singing the reprise of "Guys and Dolls." It was sort of an ensemble thing—a chance for every single one of us to sing together. Kind of a pre-finale bow. Mr. Romeo had come up with this bit all by himself, and was very proud of it.

The Mission Choir Director, Lieutenant Agatha, was supposed to call to us to get our attention before belting out the first line. Miranda stood where Mr. Romeo had put her, but when she opened her mouth, something bad came out. Not like something bad came out of my mouth during auditions, but a bad noise. Something that started out as a note, and ended up sounding like a frog sneezing. Something that decidedly did *not* sound like Miranda Goetz.

During the last week, Miranda's voice had been getting progressively scratchier, but she was usually able to get it under control. She was always armed with mugs of teas and throat sprays and honey-mint drops, and given a few minutes, she usually got her voice back in form. But this time it was different. Her voice sounded . . . broken. Miranda realized it right away. She stood, frozen, holding her hands at her throat like it might help if we couldn't see it.

No one seemed to know what to do. Savannah, who was standing right next to me, nudged my elbow and raised one eyebrow. Andrew nodded like he was a fortune-teller who'd predicted this very moment. I noticed to my astonishment that Delilah, standing center stage, had something like a sneer on her face.

It was Tucker who first broke the mass paralysis. He walked over to Miranda and put his hand on her shoulder, speaking quietly to her. Mr. Romeo quickly joined them, and the three of them stood, huddled and speaking inaudibly. Both seemed to be trying to comfort Miranda, who kept rubbing her throat and looking surprised, like something had just jumped down it and taken up residence without her permission. I was selfish enough to feel jealous at the attention Tucker was paying to Miranda. Why didn't anything terrible ever happen to me when he was around? I briefly imagined accidentally falling off the stage and breaking my leg—the OOMA rushing to my side and clasping *my* shoulder—murmuring quiet, reassuring things to *me* as the rest of the Drama Club stood by helpless.

Miranda ribbeted audibly, and seemed about to cry. Mr. Romeo spoke quietly to her, nodding his head to reassure her of something. Miranda nodded back, then walked to the edge of the stage and hopped down by the front row of seats. Tucker hopped down after her. She gathered up her large bag, which Tucker took from her. Head hanging, Miranda headed for the back exit at full speed. And Tucker, picking up the rest of her things, followed her. As the door shut behind them, the cast remained almost completely silent. I snuck a peek at Harper, sitting in her customary spot at the director's table out in the seats. She caught my eye, then quickly looked away. I looked away too. I didn't want Harper to see me right now. I was bursting with curiosity and I'm sure it showed, and to be horribly honest, I was more curious about what Tucker said to Miranda than about the details of what had just happened to her voice. He was carrying her bag for her!

Mr. Romeo stood for a moment with his hands on his hips. He looked like the worried coach in a football team underdog movie. Then he seemed to get his moxie back, and he clapped loudly a few times and raised his voice into the zone of the first soprano.

"People. People! Gather round, please."

It was easier said than done, but the cast moved en masse to the very edge of the stage. Some of the Hot Box Girls stage left had to push and wiggle through, and they were still stuck behind a row of high rollers. The Mission Choir, on the other hand, had a great view of Mr. Romeo. I was holding my breath. I wasn't sure what was happening, but whatever it was, I knew it was *highly* dramatic.

"Okay, listen up. As some of you know, Miranda Goetz has been having trouble with her vocal cords. Miss Maslin and I hoped that by giving Miranda a scaled-back part with limited lines and singing, she'd be able to participate in this production. Sadly, it seems that this has simply been too taxing for Miranda's voice. We could not have foreseen this, but Miranda has decided and I agree that she simply cannot go on."

A series of gasps and murmurs erupted. One of the gasps came out of my mouth. Lots of disembodied voices floated around asking the same basic question, "What are we going to do?" Mr. Romeo had combined several parts, including "Mission Choir Director," into Agatha's role, so though it was a small one, there were more than a few lines, some solo singing bits, and a lot of important blocking. It was a smallish part, but a Real Part. A Real Part that I happened to have memorized, courtesy of Mia Kezdekian. I had known it all along! I was never destined to be an anonymous body in the Mission Choir. I was better than that, and now I was going to get the part to prove it.

"People, quiet down please. We have some important decisions to make. Now, clearly this is a setback, but one from which we can certainly recover. We're going to have to replace Miranda with a new actress.

We may need to schedule an extra run-through or two, but there is time to work this out if we move quickly. Are we agreed?"

People were nodding and making comments that no one could hear. Still center stage, Delilah Fortescue raised her hand.

"Yes, Delilah?" Mr. Romeo said.

"I completely agree, Mr. Romeo," Delilah said. "And while I feel devastated for Miranda, I know we need to replace her as soon as possible. As president of the Drama Club and as a lead in this production, I've interacted with most of the actors and actresses, even the new ones. I think it makes sense that Miranda's replacement come from the Mission Choir since they are in all of Miranda's scenes, and based on how I've seen them work, I have a suggestion for who should be chosen."

My heart started hammering in my chest. The hammering then moved down into my stomach and churned everything I'd eaten that day into a frothy, nauseating brew. I could hardly believe what was going to happen. How had I ever doubted that Delilah was my friend?

"I think the new Lieutenant Agatha should be Savannah."

Huh?

Did I hear her correctly? *Savannah?* The Blond

Cherubic Newbie? But Delilah had come to my *house*! Delilah had noticed that I had theatrical training. She said I was the only one who knew what I was doing. I stared at her dumbly.

Delilah looked right through me for a second, then she turned to Mia and gave her a sly bug-eyed smile. What was she thinking—had she lost her mind?

"Interesting, Delilah," said Mr. Romeo. "Thank you. Savannah? What do you think?"

Everybody was looking at Savannah, and I desperately tried to rearrange my face into a casual expression, because I was sure people were looking at me too. Thank goodness Tucker had left the auditorium. Did I look as confused as I felt? Did I look like I thought I deserved the part more than Savannah? I could feel a blush starting in my cheeks. I didn't know where to look or how to act, so I stared blankly at Savannah. Her whole face had come alive with excitement, and hope, and maybe a little nausea because she might, just might, be about to get a little speaking part in *Guys and Dolls* even though she was only a seventh grader. Her chipmunk cheeks were pink, and her hands were trembling. And her eyes were absolutely glowing. I could tell she was way too nervous to speak up, to say anything on her own behalf, but I could also tell that she wanted that part. Really wanted it. Just like me.

"I have a suggestion too," came a cool voice.

Everyone turned to looked at Mia Kezdekian.

"Phoebe's ahead of the game," Mia said. "She already knows the part—the lines and blocking both."

And suddenly everybody was looking at *me*. Except for Mia, who was giving Delilah a triumphant if unpleasant smile. Delilah scowled back at her.

"Phoebe?" Mr. Romeo asked. He was frowning with such concentration, his silver eyebrows had fused together in one line. "Do you know the lines and blocking?"

"Mr. Romeo, I really think that Savannah—" Delilah began.

He silenced her just by raising one hand in the air, palm facing out. Neat trick, that.

"Phoebe?" Mr. Romeo repeated.

It was like the world's most enormous spotlight was on me. I was so close to getting what I wanted. If I opened my mouth right now and admitted that I knew Miranda's part backwards and forwards, Mr. Romeo would probably give it to me in spite of Delilah's recommendation. And I wanted that part. I truly, madly, and deeply wanted to play Lieutenant Agatha. But everything was happening so fast. I needed to think before I opened my mouth.

I looked around the stage. Delilah and Mia were

still glaring at each other. And then I finally understood. How stupid I'd been to think that either of them had "chosen" me because they thought I was special. They were just using me to swat at each other. I was no better than a tennis ball.

But what did all that matter now if I ended up with the part? What did I care if it gave Mia a victory over Delilah? They weren't my friends, and probably never would be. It was only about the part now. All I had to do was confirm that I had memorized it, which I had, and everybody would be happy. Except maybe Savannah. Savannah's name had been suggested first. If Mia hadn't opened her mouth, the issue would already be settled. If I was going to take it, I was going to have to steal it from under Savannah's feet. I looked over at her.

"Phoebe?" Mr. Romeo repeated.

Savannah stood silently next to me, staring at her feet. Her lower lip looked like it might be trying to stifle a quiver. A tiny blond curl had floated out over her eyebrow, and I wanted to reach over and flick it out of the way. I had a pretty good feeling what was going on inside her head. She wanted the part just as much as I did. But she wasn't going to jump in and pounce on it. She wasn't going to go head-to-head with me.

Then I peeked out at the director's table. Harper

was sitting up very straight, watching me. She looked worried and a little confused, like she had when she'd first read about the Ebola virus. I had taken so many steps away from Harper these past few weeks. And it had all happened after I met Delilah and Mia, when I wanted to be just like them and started thinking that being friends with those girls made me special. Standing there onstage, with every living soul in the Drama Club staring at me, suddenly all I wanted in the world was to have Harper back. Or else, to refuse to give her up without a fight.

"No, Mr. Romeo," I heard myself saying. "Sorry. I don't know the part."

Mr. Romeo sighed.

"Well, we need to move on. Savannah, what do you think about this? Do you want to take a crack at playing Lieutenant Agatha?"

Savannah stood there, frozen like a deer in the headlights. Andrew was nudging her and saying something, but she wasn't looking at Andrew. She was looking at me. Did she think she needed my permission? Maybe that was the message I'd been giving her all this time—that she needed to accept I was above her in the pecking order. But I knew I wasn't above Savannah. Actually, I suspected we probably had a whole lot in common. Savannah's pale blue eyes began to water, and her little blond eyebrows dived into a worried frown. I imagined us together throughout the years, working on shows, all the experiences we'd have—the parts we would play. Had Delilah and Mia started out like this, head-to-head over a part? Did either of them have any real friends now?

"Go for it," I whispered to Savannah.

And in spite of worrying that I looked stupid, I gave Savannah an encouraging grin and a thumbs-up sign.

The smile Savannah shot back my way was blinding. A smile like that had to hurt. I know it hurt *me*. But it also felt good.

"Savannah?" Mr. Romeo asked.

"Yes, Mr. Romeo, I'm up for it. I can play Lieutenant Agatha."

"Are you sure, Savannah? You'll need to have the lines and blocking down by tomorrow."

"I'll help her," I said. "I know the— I'd be happy to run lines with her."

"Excellent. We have a new Lieutenant Agatha. Congratulations, Savannah," said Mr. Romeo.

Savannah made a little gasping noise, like sometimes the contestants on *Jeopardy!* do when they get a big question right. She looked over at me and made a little spastic fanning motion in front of her heart with her hand that I knew meant many things, including "Oh my gosh I can't believe it thank you so much oh my gosh!"

Then before I knew it, Savannah had locked me in a Killer Chipmunk hug. Over her shoulder, I looked out into the seats. Mr. Romeo had gone over to the director's table and was talking to Harper. But briefly, she looked up and caught my eye. And before she looked away again, she gave me a small smile. At least I think she did. Maybe I imagined it. I let Savannah hug me for all she was worth, and I even gave her a bit of a squeeze back.

Who knew? I actually sort of liked chipmunks.

Believe it or not, there was a little more drama to come at that rehearsal. We ran Lieutenant Agatha's scenes with a quietly excited Savannah clutching her script and doing the part several times, and I have to say I was impressed. She even asked me for advice a few times, which was pretty flattering. No, she didn't have the lines memorized, but she knew the part well, and she did it both following Miranda's blocking and adding something uniquely of her own. Savannah was a good actress.

When rehearsal was finally wrapping up, I went over to the seat where I'd left my bookbag. Harper had already left, probably because she needed to make the school bus. I went through my bag making sure I had all the books I needed, when something made me look up toward the back of the auditorium. The door was just swinging closed, and I could see my mother standing there. She was supposed to pick me up in the parking lot. Why was she in here? When she started walking I realized instantly that it was not me but Mr. Romeo she was heading for. I suddenly knew exactly why she was here.

When I'd had my crying fit the other night, I had never told my mother about my fight with Harper. I had left her with the impression that I was crying about having to play Spin the Bottle. Now here she was in the flesh, marching toward Mr. Romeo with all the resolve of a knight on crusade. My mother was going to spill the beans about Spin the Bottle, and she was going to demand that it stop. And I knew she was going to do this not to be mean, or desperately uncool, or controlling, but she was going to do it because she honestly felt I was upset about it. And that other students might be upset about it too. She was trying to help. But what she was actually going to do was Ruin My Life.

I dropped my bag with a thud, and bounded across the auditorium, climbing over three rows of chairs, to intercept my mother before she could reach Mr. Romeo.

"Mom," I hissed. Then, realizing the need for volume, I yelled. "MOM!"

She stopped, surprised but compliant. I ignored the various heads turning in my direction, and struggled over a few rows until I had reached her.

"Mom, listen. Let's go outside—let's go to the car."

She frowned in confusion.

"Honey, I really need to talk to your director. If you'd like to listen in, then you're welcome, but this issue has got to be addressed, Phoebe. Opening night is only a week or so away."

"Mom, please," I said. "If you want to be helpful right now, and I know that you *do*, then you'll come outside with me. We can talk in the car. Mom. It's important. Please."

I give my mother credit for the fact that when I tell her something is important, she listens. She'll put aside her questions for later, and she might not ultimately agree, but when I say something is important, she gives me the benefit of the doubt.

So we turned and walked toward the door, and I knew that once we were safely outside I would tell her everything—about the fight with Harper, about Delilah and Mia and how they had used me, and how the Blond Cherubic Newbie had just gotten a big promotion. I wasn't looking forward to spilling my guts, but I wasn't exactly dreading it either. My mother occasionally had some not-so-bad advice to offer. And at least she'd understand that it was not the game of Spin the Bottle that had been upsetting me—that she didn't need to go in with guns blazing to shut it down. Because now there wasn't a reason to. You'll understand, then, why I thought it best not to tell her about the OOMA.

As my mother walked up the aisle ahead of me, I realized she was wearing the tracksuit that said "SMILE" on the butt.

And what else could I do?

I smiled.

CHAPTER TWELVE

Chilling with Tonky Butt

That night, I was finally able to retreat to my room for a little quality time with Tonky Butt. As I thought, it hadn't been too bad unloading the last few weeks on my mother, but the intense discussion in the car had kind of exhausted me. I don't know how her Talk Yoga patients did it. I was just settling in on my bed with my iPod and my favorite girl band mix when I heard a knock at the door. Predictably, my mother was in my room before I had a chance to say anything.

"Pheebs," she said with this huge smile on her face. I hoped she wasn't expecting us to do another bonding thing. A girl needed to recover.

"Pheebs, honey, guess who's downstairs."

I sat up. Several possibilities flitted through my head, none of them all that good.

"It's Harper!"

"Oh no, Mom, you didn't!" I said urgently, but keeping my voice low.

"Didn't what? I didn't do anything," my mother said, matching her tone to my quiet one.

"You mean to tell me that just a few hours after we have our big heart-to-heart and I tell you all about the fight and how my best friend and I aren't speaking, that Harper just *happens* to show up here of her own free will, with no urging or convincing from any outside source?"

My mother looked at me very hard.

"Phoebe, that's exactly what I'm telling you," she said very quietly.

Wow. Harper had decided to come see me on her own. This was great! Or was it? Maybe Harper had come to officially end our friendship in person. A formal gesture of that kind would be like her.

"Phoebe?" my mother asked. "Don't you want me to tell her to come up?"

"Yeah," I said quickly. "Of course."

My mother paused in the doorway.

"It's going to be fine, sweetie," she said. "Just be you. Harper is always going to be your friend as long as you're being you."

That sentence needed its own theme song.

"Okay," I said, a little impatiently. Therapy time was over. It was face the music time.

My mother left the room, and I pulled Tonky Butt onto my lap. I made him turn his head around and gaze up at me.

"What?" I whispered to him, squeezing his balding tail. "Just be you, Tonky Butt. No worries."

"At least one thing hasn't changed."

I looked up. Harper was standing in the doorway.

"What?"

"You still talk to Tonky Butt when you think you're alone. That's probably a good sign."

"Are you coming in?"

Harper stepped through the doorway, looking around my room like I might have changed something in the two weeks we'd not hung out.

"It's all the same," I said. "I should Swiffer, maybe. Get the crud from under the bed."

Harper hesitated, then lowered herself carefully into the beanbag chair. It made a quiet crunching sound as it conformed to her shape.

It was weird, Harper sitting there, me on the bed. So familiar. So normal. And yet I was terrified to say anything, because it might be the wrong thing. Or I might discover that there was no right thing to say, not anymore.

"Rehearsal today," Harper said.

"Yeah," I stated, replying or agreeing or maybe just showing that I was willing to talk too.

"Quite an unfolding of events," she said.

"Yeah," I repeated. I wanted to say more, but I just didn't know where Harper was going with this.

"So had you? Memorized Miranda's lines and stuff?"

"Oh. Actually, yeah. I had. I mean, you remember what Mia told me and everything. I just figured, why not."

"But you didn't say anything. When Mia said you had learned the part already, when Mr. Romeo asked. You didn't say it was true."

"Yeah." My amazing, sophisticated, widely varied vocabulary. Yeah.

"Why? Why not?"

Harper's tone hadn't changed, but she was looking at me intently. I had a feeling that this was the question she'd come to ask—that the answer was somehow very important to her. I could spend all day figuring out what it was she wanted to hear and why. In the end it didn't matter what Harper wanted to hear. All I had was the truth.

"Well, I really wanted to. I mean, you have no idea. But all these thoughts were coming to me at the same time. Everything happened so fast. When

Delilah volunteered Savannah for the part, I realized—well, I realized she was just playing around with me. What Delilah really wanted was to get one over on Mia Kezdekian. I was such an idiot to think they were so cool, Harp. I was so gullible."

Harper gave a tiny nod. I had been so irritated with the way Harper dismissed Delilah and Mia, but she'd been dead-on right.

"Those girls, they're just the opposite of everything I want to be, Harper."

"But you want to be an actress," Harper said.

"Yes," I said emphatically. "I do. I still do, more than ever. But I don't want to be *like them*."

Harper nodded thoughtfully.

"I know I spend so much time worrying how I look to other people," I continued. "I wanted the Drama Club kids to see me as one of them. And somehow in the process, I messed everything up. I'm an idiot."

Harper shook her head, leaned over toward me, and grabbed Tonky Butt out of my lap. She gave the skinny stuffed otter a long hug. After a moment, she cleared her throat.

"I've been an idiot too," Harper said. "I was . . ."

She paused and stared into Tonky Butt's eyes for encouragement. It always worked for me.

"I was jealous, Pheebs. I was really jealous.

Because you seemed to idolize those girls, and you're such a great actress—why wouldn't they love you? Why wouldn't the whole Drama Club love you? But I didn't like Delilah or Mia, and I couldn't pretend I did. And they obviously didn't even register my existence. I thought they would take you away from me."

Wow. Of everything that had gone through my mind, every way I'd analyzed our fight and what had happened to our friendship, it had never occurred to me that Harper felt jealous. That she thought Delilah would take her place! The thought of it now seemed so utterly ridiculous. How on earth had it happened?

I took a deep breath and said what I needed to say.

"That day at your house, I could tell you didn't want to talk about Delilah and Mia and the Spin the Bottle thing and all that. I knew you weren't interested, and I guess . . . You just seemed all superior or mature or whatever, and I felt kind of lame. I thought you were judging me. Then we just stopped talking, and I thought you'd decided that I was more of a *Seventeen* magazine girl and you were more of a *National Geographic* girl, and you just didn't want to be friends anymore."

Harper sighed and rubbed her forehead.

"Well . . . I guess maybe . . . I guess that's what I

did want you to think. I was afraid of the competition. And so I acted superior. You have your ways of dealing with the world, and I have mine."

Harper stopped, as if that were the end of her explanation. I cocked an eyebrow at her.

"Pretending to be all Smarter-Than-Thou really works for me," she continued, looking at her hands. "And I'm great at it. I'm Dr. Tanaka's daughter, the genius girl. If I think someone doesn't like me, I can just, you know, call them a Tiny Mind and act above it all. Then it just looks like I don't care." She stopped again, then rushed on. "I was afraid I was too boring to be your friend anymore because I didn't want to play Spin the Bottle. When you didn't call, I figured it was a done deal."

"Are you kidding? I was waiting for *you* to call *me!*" I said.

There was a pause. Then at the precise same moment, we both burst into laughter. I didn't feel like crying anymore.

"I think I'm starting to get it," I said. "We've always been like two parts of the same person, Harp. But now that we're in middle school, I think we're not always—I think we're starting to find places where we don't always fit with each other so perfectly. But that doesn't mean we can't still be best friends. We're just . . ."

"Diversifying," Harper said.

"Exactly," I said, even though I didn't really know what that word meant. Harper said it so convincingly, I was certain it was accurate.

"We don't have to love all the same things all the time, or do all the same things together," Harper added. "And if one of us is into something new, the other one doesn't have to take it as a threat."

"You said it, sister," I replied. Then more tentatively, I asked, "So, we're okay?"

"We're more than okay," Harper exclaimed. And she came over and threw her arms around me, which is big, because Harper isn't a natural born hugger. I squeezed back hard, a little chipmunk move I learned from the BCN.

"More than okay," Harper repeated, gently wiggling loose of my clutch.

I took a deep, happy sigh. The relief was enormous, and I wanted to do everything at once: work on the comic strip, go to Harper's for a sleep-over, do my impression of the barrel-chested French teacher. Oh, and I needed some serious help in math.

"How long did you guys keep rehearsing after I left?" Harper asked.

"Until five. Oh, you won't believe this, Harp. We were just wrapping things up, and I look over and see my mother marching down the aisle like Attila the Hun invading a small country. What *is* a Hun anyway?"

"A nomadic Asian tribe during the Dark Ages. So what was she doing?"

"One of those terminally concerned PTA moms told her about opening night Spin the Bottle. I'd been, you know . . . pretty bummed because of you and me and all that. And she thought I was stressed out because of the game—that I was being pressured to do something that was psychologically damaging me!"

"Not likely," Harper said with a snort.

"I know, right? So she's about to create a level of personal humiliation that will dog me all the rest of my school years by confronting Mr. Romeo and demanding he put a stop to the game. Somehow I managed to intercept her and convince her that I didn't need her to fix this particular situation."

"Did you tell her you actually wanted to play?" Harper asked, grinning.

"Please. No, I gave her a beautiful speech in which I promised that I would not be pressured in either direction, and that I would not do anything that I felt I didn't want to do."

"A technical truth!"

"A technical truth," I said, grinning. "So I can play if I want to. That is, if there even is a game this year."

"Why wouldn't there be?"

I shrugged.

"I don't know—I got the impression Delilah is totally boss of the game. You know, she's the one always talking it up, telling the new kids about it, whispering about it when Mr. Romeo can't hear—"

"Doing her wink," Harper added.

I laughed.

"Right! The wink! Anyway, my mother in her shrink-tastic wisdom offered the theory that Delilah is kind of a control freak. You know, like she has to be in charge and move people around like chess pieces, but she doesn't really care about any of them. She's president of the Drama Club and she runs the Spin the Bottle game, and it seems like maybe that's another way she can control people. And if she loses control of people, she can't deal. So I heard Delilah and Bud arguing a few days ago, and from the tiny bit I heard she was essentially forbidding him to play Spin the Bottle on opening night since he is now her boyfriend and technically off-limits. I mean, what girl wants to play a game where her boyfriend might kiss some other chick?"

"Like Mia Kezdekian," Harper said.

I squealed.

"Exactly! Anyway, my theory is that Bud is staging a little rebellion. He's not going to let Delilah stop him from playing, and now that I think of it, I doubt he's going to stand by and let her cancel the game."

"And Delilah is Not Pleased," Harper said, grinning.

"Exactly. So who knows. Either there will be a game, or there won't. Which means the OOMA . . . Oh, you don't even know!"

"Know what?" Harper asked.

I gave her a highly detailed account of the Mountain Dew Incident. I acted out what I'd said, then acted out what Tucker had said. I even let Harper hold the Mountain Dew can so she could fully appreciate the vibes.

"And he never got around to asking this question?"

"No!" I cried. "It's probably nothing, right? It probably didn't mean anything."

Harper looked extremely, deeply, atom-splittingly thoughtful. I watched her breathlessly. Finally, she shook her head.

"No? No you don't think it means anything?"

"No, I *do*," Harper said. "It's . . . guys are like a totally different species, granted. But they're not *stupid*. If a guy is standing alone with a girl and it's even remotely apparent that she's crushing on him, he's not going to stammer and blush and tell her he'd like to ask her something if it isn't significant. That'd be like a doctor telling a patient to sit down and prepare themselves, when he's about to tell them that all they have is a bad cold."

"Wait . . . so what are you saying?" I asked eagerly.

"It's Occam's Razor," Harper said.

I nodded patiently, and when I couldn't take it anymore, I yelled, "I don't know what that IS!"

"Sorry," Harper said. "Occam's Razor is a scientific principal that essentially says that the simplest solution to a puzzle is statistically the most likely one to be accurate. That if it seemed like Tucker was going to ask you a boy/girl-related question, the most likely reason is that he *was*."

I sank back on the bed, the world spinning.

"He might actually really like me?"

"He might actually really like you," Harper said. "And why shouldn't he?"

I saw no point in presenting an alphabetical list of the reasons Tucker Wells might not really like me. Harper, genius daughter of Dr. Tanaka, with the help of Occam's Comb or Toothbrush or whatever, thought that he *might*. And for the moment, that was good enough for me.

"And listen. I'll go with you to the game, Phoebe. I still don't want to play, but you can count on me for moral support. If you want."

I beamed and nodded, and my face got all hot.

Delilah was a Tiny Mind, the OOMA might really like me, and Harper was back.

All was right with the world, and I was ready as I'd ever be for opening night.

CHAPTER THIRTEEN

Final. Dress. Rehearsal.

The energy in the auditorium for final dress rehearsal was out of control. I personally could barely contain my excitement and terror. There was a frenzy of activity everywhere. Lou was onstage hammering some last-minute nails. Three of the Hot Box Girls were standing nervously in line to have their costumes re-hemmed. Chris Seligman, in zoot suit costume but still wearing his own jet-black scarf, was pacing and clearing his throat repeatedly while mumbling through his lines. Ben Pfeiffer appeared to be reenacting a video he'd seen on MTV, while Fedora Kravitz watched, entranced. I didn't see Delilah or Bud anywhere, and wondered if they had special star dressing rooms with air-conditioning and easy chairs, where they reclined away from the riffraff in the chorus and the stage crew. Or maybe they were out back, arguing.

Somebody tapped me on the shoulder. I turned and beheld the glory that is Mia Kezdekian.

Dressed for her first "Adelaide and the Hot Box Girls" dance number, Mia looked . . . breathtaking. Less gorgeous girls had their own calendars. Her leotard dress glittered and rippled with her every move; her black hair was piled up on her head with several wisps artfully curled around her face; she even had an actual feather boa—pink—draped around her neck. She couldn't have come from the regular world like the rest of us. It was almost as if she came from . . . Hollywood.

"So," Mia said, glancing up and down at my military-style Salvation Army costume, below-the-knee navy blue skirt and matching jacket, fastened clear up to my neck with large brass buttons. Sexy? I think not.

"You blew it. You could have had Miranda's part."

Ah, there it was. Until now, neither Mia nor Delilah had said anything to me in the days following Savannah's ascension to Lieutenant Agatha. Actually, I never noticed Mia really talking to anyone, except to make the occasional barbed remark about

Delilah during rehearsal. She didn't seem to have any friends. Which would make her as flawed as any of the rest of us.

"I wouldn't say I blew it," I replied. "I made a decision, that's all."

"What decision was there to make?" Mia shot back. "You could have stepped up and grabbed the part, become important. But you faked out, you got scared. So you're still stuck in the chorus with the babies."

There was so much I could have said. Mia had practically offered me a pedestal from which to deliver her a blistering moral speech. But really, who cared? I knew who I was, and what I'd done, and why. If Mia wanted to think I'd simply chickened out, what difference did it make?

For the first time in my life, what someone else thought of me did not matter.

Mia was still standing there, her spectacular lips half pursed. I just shrugged.

"I guess I misjudged you," Mia said coldly.

"Yeah, there's a lot of that going around these days," I replied.

She looked blank for a moment.

"Anyway," Mia finally said. Then she walked away.

"Phee!"

It was Savannah, bearing down on me with the brightness and force of a solar flare.

"I'm terrified! Are you terrified? Is this really happening? Phee, I'm freaking out!"

I patted Savannah on the arm.

"Relax. You're going to be fine!" I told her. Which she one day might learn meant she was not in immediate danger of dying, or causing another to die.

"I feel a little nauseous," Savannah said, clutching one of my elbows in her Chipmunk Death Grip.

"Everybody does, a little," I said knowingly. "Don't worry about it. Let's just have fun! Anyway, it's not like it's opening night. It's just final dress rehearsal. Only a tiny audience—they have to be personally invited by Mr. Romeo."

Savannah turned pale.

"There's an audience tonight?"

"No, not really," I said, trying to sound reassuring. "Just a couple people. Some random faces. An audience-lette. Don't you trust Mr. Romeo?"

"Completely," Savannah said, with a touch of reverence in her voice.

"Okay, then," I said, gently disentangling myself from her grip.

"Okay," Savannah repeated. "Phoebe, I could NOT do this without you."

"You probably could," I said, smiling. But it was nice of her to say.

"Oh, I almost forgot what I came to tell you!"

Savannah cried. "I didn't know if you'd heard."

"Heard what?" I asked.

"About the Spin the Bottle problem. Some PTA mom found out about it and went postal."

"Somebody's *mom*? Found *out*? About the *game*?" I cried, trying to look astonished and scandalized.

"Yeah, apparently this PTA mom is starting some peer pressure group or something, and even though her kid isn't in Drama Club she called Mr. Romeo and made a lot of noise. He didn't flat out make us promise not to do it, because he said . . . how did he put it? It wasn't in his purview. Don't you just LOVE him? Anyway, he did tell us that the PTA is going to have people, basically like undercover chaperones, around on opening night. There's no way they'll let the game happen."

I should have realized that just because my mother let it go, the issue was not over. Some *other* mother had gone all Attila the Hun. This was nuts! All the worrying, and wondering, and okay . . . practicing with the orange.

In fact, I had planned my entire morning tomorrow around the ritual of lip softening, flossing, exfoliating my face, and frequent and aggressive breath freshening. I thought I would have hours to run through each possible Spin the Bottle scenario in my head, and to rehearse each one. What to do if

Scooter Nemo's bottle pointed at me. What to do if my bottle pointed at Ben Pfeiffer. How to act if (perish the thought) Mia's bottle pointed at Tucker. I couldn't bring myself to even imagine that Tucker's bottle would do anything so treacherous as point at Mia. Then there was the question of perfume (What kind? How much?) and hair style (Up or down? Dangly earrings or studs?). Expression questions. When to smile? Or eyes-only smile? Mysterious expression? And back to the lips. I was planning to apply Burt's Bees Lip Balm every half hour from the time I got out of bed to the call for places on opening night. I'd even found a tiny pocket on my costume that could allow me to carry the tube with me at all times. All for nothing?

"The game's not called off or anything," Savannah added.

Oh.

"It's just rescheduled. To . . . are you ready for this? *Tonight!* After the final dress rehearsal, in the prop room."

Savannah stared at me, wide-eyed, and I stared back. I had a feeling my eyes were kind of saucer-sized too.

"So, are you gonna go, Phee? Because I'll go if you go. Are you?"

I took a deep breath. This was not the way I

thought it was going to happen. I wasn't ready to play Spin the Bottle today. But if the game had been rescheduled, then I would have to reschedule right along with it.

"Yeah, I'm gonna go," I said. I tried to sound casual, but I could hear a quiver in my voice. Savannah drowned it out by squealing as soon as I got out the word *yeah*. She clapped her hands in excitement.

"Yay! I've gotta get backstage. You're the best, Phee!"

"Savannah!" I called. She'd already started to dash away. The girl moved faster than any living creature I had ever seen.

"Yeah?" she called back.

I was going to tell her that my nickname was Pheebs. But the excited and happy look Savannah was shooting my way gave me pause. Why not just let her call me Phee? It wasn't too totally uncute, as nicknames went, and who was to say I couldn't have more than one nickname, now that I had more than one friend?

"Have an awesome show."

Savannah shot me a hockey puck–sized grin.

"You too, Phee!"

Then she was off like a shot, and I knew we were getting close to curtain time.

"People!" came the clarion call that seemed to have no exact point of origin. "We're at ten minutes. That means five minutes for your call to places. Remember, we are proceeding with this final run-through exactly as if it were an actual performance with audience. We go straight through the show, no stopping. I don't care if you forget a line, miss an entrance, or collide with a piece of the set. Just. Keep. Going."

I caught sight of Mr. Romeo, standing near the front row in all his glory. He looked bathed in celestial light. As I was looking at him, I saw Harper dash over and whisper something to him. Thunderclouds suddenly shadowed his scrubbed and cleanly shaven face.

"People! Has anyone seen Tucker Wells? Tucker Wells?"

Oh no. NO! Had the OOMA, the kindhearted, lusciously attractive boy of my dreams, neglected to show up for final dress rehearsal? This crisis forced all thoughts of Spin the Bottle entirely out of my brain.

I felt short of breath as I looked around anxiously. Mr. Romeo was again asking if anyone had seen Tucker. I knew I hadn't. I never saw Tucker without having the experience seared into my brain in excruciating detail.

"You'd have noticed if he was here, right?"

In my panic, I hadn't even realized Harper had run over to me. I gave her a panic-stricken look.

"What's going to happen to him? What's going to happen to the show? Liver Lips Louie has lines and everything!"

Harper shook her head.

"I don't know. They'll have to wing it. This is terrible!"

"But he wouldn't do it on purpose, Harp. You know how he is. He spaces on things all the time. He'd never deliberately blow something like this off."

"I know," Harper said, looking worried, "but the unfortunate reality is that—"

I heard a door bang, and something like a meteor whizzed through the room. A meteor with floppy hair that was shouting "SORRY!"

I clutched Harper with both hands.

"There he is. He's here!"

I hung on to her as I watched Mr. Romeo stride over to Tucker, who was totally out of breath from his sprint. I don't know what Mr. Romeo said, but he glowered so intensely, he created a crevasse in his forehead. Tucker was nodding and looking humble and contrite. Then Mr. Romeo pointed backstage, in the direction of the costume room, and Tucker took off running again. He had about three minutes to transform himself into Liver Lips Louie. I could have wept with relief.

I was already in full costume and makeup and ready to go. I stood stock-still. A billion thoughts seemed to be charging through my head.

"Pheebs, it's three minutes 'til places. You should be onstage. Are you okay?"

Several Harpers clutching several clipboards seemed to be swimming before my eyes. People were starting to filter into the auditorium—Mr. Romeo's audience-lette. I held on to Harper's arm.

"Do you feel sick?" she whispered, her brown eyes going wide with alarm.

I shook my head. I didn't feel sick, not the way Harper meant. I was actually feeling relatively calm about the dress rehearsal. But now that Tucker had safely arrived, the specter of Spin the Bottle had returned to wig me out. All my planning had been for nothing, and I was supposed to accept that I had to play Spin the Bottle *tonight*. In, like, a matter of *hours*. No practicing. No Burt's Bees. Yikes, had I even flossed this morning? I had absolutely no way to get fresh breath, or even recently freshened breath. Could I risk kissing someone with stale breath? It could go horribly wrong! This was tragic. A catastrophe of oral hygiene.

"They had to change Spin the Bottle to tonight!" I whispered.

Harper's mouth dropped open.

"But you . . . "

I nodded.

"Oh Pheebs, I promised to be there with you for moral support. But I can't tonight! There's this physics salon downtown after the show and I promised my dad I would be there because he's heading a talk on string theory and I'm supposed to help out and we've had it planned for like, forever—"

I squeezed her arm.

"You know what? It's okay, Harp. The Blond . . . Savannah is going to go. And . . . I think this is something I can do. Seriously. I'll be fine."

I will not be in danger of immediately dying, or causing someone else to die.

Harper looked genuinely stricken, like she might cry.

"Places!" Mr. Romeo sang. "Cast, it is now time for places!"

Harper rummaged through her pocket, and pressed something into my hand, then sprinted in the direction of the lighting/director's booth. I looked at what she'd put in my hand.

A roll of peppermint Life Savers.

Harper had saved my life.

"I'll call you!" I yelled after her.

She turned back to give me the thumbs-up while

she was still running. I made the international thumb/pinkie-to-ear sign for "telephone" and nodded vigorously. Then I hustled up the stairs and behind the curtain. When I got to the place I was supposed to be standing when the lights went up, Savannah whispered something to me, and gently moved my arm down to my side.

I had been standing in place with my Harper-handphone still in place, pinkie at the mouth, thumb at the ear, a roll of Life Savers tucked into my palm.

Like, can you hear me now?

CHAPTER FOURTEEN

Spinning the Bottle

The final dress rehearsal itself was something of a blur. I'm pretty sure that I, personally, made no mistakes. I do know that in our big Mission scene, when Sergeant Sarah had one dozen certified sinners attending her prayer meeting, that something went wrong during Nicely Nicely's song "Sit Down, You're Rocking the Boat." It was Kelvin Black's big solo, and the Mission Choir was supposed to add little background harmonies and business every once in a while. When Kelvin sang "a great big wave came and washed me overboard," the entire Mission Choir was supposed to stand up by the pews and shriek "heeeeeeeeeeeeellllp!" Only, Dana came in a verse early, when Kelvin was still singing about bringing his dice along. She got to her feet, raised one hand high in the air, and screamed "Heeelll," then abruptly sat down, managing to save only the *p* sound for later, which almost made it sound like she was screaming that Nicely Nicely was going to hell. And Delilah messed up her lines a few times. Like she just didn't know what she was supposed to be saying. Plus, three of the zoot-suited guys, including, if you must know, Liver Lips Louie, stepped back too far during the final dice game and stood on the painted backdrop, which promptly detached from the grid and slipped down onto their heads. Romalla Lee Um chose the wrong moment to go to the ladies' room, and missed an entire scene in which she had two lines. Oh, and one of the Hot Box Girls fell off the stage during a dance number.

Other than that, you know, things went fairly well. When Mr. Romeo gathered us around for notes after the run-through, he seemed fairly pleased.

"Remember, people, a bumpy final dress rehearsal makes for a flawless opening night," he said. "That's always the way it goes. Actors playing Harry the Horse, Liver Lips Louie, and Angie the Ox, I'd like you to double-check the positioning of that backdrop, please, so we don't have a repeat collapse tomorrow night. Romalla, please check with the assistant stage manager before responding to a call of nature, to confirm you have enough time. Fedora, did you hurt yourself?"

Fedora was the Hot Box Girl who'd toppled over the edge of the stage.

She shook her head. Her curls did seem slightly askew.

"Again, I'd like you to go ahead and run through your blocking there, Fedora. Maybe all the Hot Box Girls should do the same thing. We don't want to plummet into Mom and Dad's laps on opening night."

Certainly not.

"Delilah? Were there a few line issues?" Even Mr. Romeo's questions sounded super-clean, like the words went through scrubbing bubbles as they came out of his mouth.

Delilah was sitting on the edge of the stage, with her arms folded over her chest like a defiant kinder-gartner.

"There was some backstage noise that was very distracting. It blew my concentration."

She looked around at the cast with a slight air of disdain, like she was daring anyone to argue with her.

"The Mission Choir tends to be real chatty before their entrances. Voices carry, you know," Delilah finished.

Wow. No one else had blamed their mess-ups on anyone else. Even poor Fedora Kravitz, who'd plunged three feet to the auditorium floor and saved herself by landing in push-up position, hadn't blamed the accident on anyone but herself. Our leading lady, Dame Delilah, was *not* a team player.

But then, I already knew that.

When the notes were finally over, Mr. Romeo congratulated everyone and began tidily placing his notes into a gleaming leather satchel. Maybe he felt my eyes on him, or maybe it was a coincidence, but he looked up at me suddenly, then made a little sideways bob of his head. That was a Mr. Romeo-ism for "Come over here for a moment—I'd like a word."

My stomach gave a spasm even as I got up and started toward him. What could be wrong? I was sure I hadn't made any goofs in the show. Was my energy off?

"Hi," I said.

Mr. Romeo waited until he'd pulled on his overcoat, like he didn't feel a person should have any distractions while they were speaking. Then he looked intently at me—a vintage Mr. Romeo look—intently peering over the reading glasses, but impossible to interpret.

"Nice job tonight, Phoebe," he said.

My mouth almost dropped open, but I intercepted the impulse just in time.

"Oh! I mean, thank you!"

Mr. Romeo nodded.

"For the record, I was completely confident you could have stepped up to Lieutenant Agatha, had that been necessary. Savannah was quite good too, and I'm very pleased with her work. But you could have done it. I'm looking forward to directing you in the next show. I have a feeling I'm going to see some great things from you."

Then he gave another little nod, and swept away grandly like a diplomat en route to the United Nations.

I wanted to scream with excitement. Even from the far reaches of the chorus, Mr. Romeo had noticed me! Predicted great things for me! I was so wild with the thrill of his compliment, I actually forgot about what was coming up until I saw Dana and Romalla whispering together and giggling with hysterical nervousness.

It was time.

I ripped open the roll of peppermint Life Savers and crammed two into my mouth. Fedora Kravitz was brushing her hair while simultaneously shooting sparking looks in Ben Pfeiffer's direction. Annabelle was fluttering her hands in the air and hissing, "You guys! Come on. Come ON!" Mia was leaning up against the proscenium wall, looking detached and stunning. Ben and Tyler pretended to check each other's hair, then Tyler made a huge deal of smelling under his arm. Ew.

"I can't believe we're doing this," came Savannah's voice. She had a way of sneaking up on me that was truly mystifying. I took a cautious sniff of the air, then looked at her.

"You smell good. You smell really really good!"

Savannah beamed, and fished around in her purse. She pulled out a miniature bottle, burgundy-colored with a gold top.

"It's 'Lauren.' I got a sample at Bloomie's over the weekend. Want a squirt?"

Did I ever. I stood patiently like a horse being groomed as Savannah spritzed the heavenly scent over me. Practically swooning with gratitude, I offered her a Life Saver.

"Oh, YAY!" she exclaimed.

"I'm having two," I said, so Savannah doubled up as well.

"All right, dudes and chicks, are we *up* for this?" Bud Gelcho shouted.

Delilah, standing right next to him, began whispering furiously, but Bud simply started walking toward the prop room stairs. Everyone started to follow. The combination of the giggles, whispering, and the occasional squeal sounded like background noise from a kids' morning TV show.

"Here we go," I said to Savannah. She gave me a quick Chipmunk Death Grip, and the two of us, smelling like roses, headed for the stairs.

The prop room was one of a series of rooms that had been built, like the dressing rooms and costume shop, under the stage area. The prop room door was partially open, and I could hear laughter and loud talking from inside. Kelvin Black and Scooter Nemo were walking in right ahead of us.

Savannah and I looked at each other.

"Ready?" she asked.

No. No. No.

"Or should we wait just one minute? To prepare?"

"One minute," I agreed, thankfully.

"Hey Phoebe, hey Savannah. I guess this means I'm not late for once."

Tucker had come up right behind us.

"What happened to you?" I cried, forgetting for once to be on guard and studying his every movement. "I thought you were actually going to miss the dress rehearsal. Then I thought Mr. Romeo was going to fire you!"

Tucker gave me a lopsided grin.

"It's nuts. I put on this old Timex watch today after school, because I'd lost it and then it just showed up at the back of my sock drawer. It's a cool watch. But I haven't worn it since spring, and . . . " Tucker started to chuckle. "The battery was running out. I was more than an hour off."

"That is the craziest thing I ever heard," I declared. "Tucker, pick a watch and stick with it. Preferably something accurate. Something Swiss."

"I know, right?" he said, still grinning. My knees weakened slightly.

"So you didn't get fired?" Savannah asked.

"Actually, I kind of did," Tucker replied. "Not for this show. But Mr. Romeo said I'm banned from acting in the spring production."

"No!" I cried. "That's not fair!"

"It's okay," Tucker said. "It actually is kind of more than fair, if you think about it. He could have kicked me out of Drama Club. I showed up three minutes before curtain of final dress. That's uncool. Anyway, I'm not banned from working on the set in the spring, and I could use the extra time for my homework. So really. It's okay."

I took a deep breath.

"So what do we think about all this?" Tucker asked, inclining his head toward the prop room door. He was talking to both of us, but he was looking at me.

Gulp.

"What do *you* think?" I asked, stalling for time. Was this The Question? Was there meaning here, or only my active imagination?

"I usually play," Tucker said. "But I've never been . . . I mean, it's more complicated this year because I kind of . . . "

He gave an agonized glance in Savannah's direction and lowered his voice.

"Because I kind of . . . like someone this year, you know?"

And though he didn't say anything else, I knew. Just by the way he was looking at me, and the pink shade his face had turned. The OOMA liked me. He *liked* me.

Suddenly, a yell came from the prop room, the unmistakable platoon-sergeant bellow of Delilah Fortescue.

"Last call. This door closes in THIRTY SEC-ONDS, and no one enters or leaves after that. LAST CALL!"

Savannah squeezed my arm. She looked positively green.

"You're coming in with me, right?" she whispered.

Tucker and I exchanged a look.

"I promised her," I said. "That we'd go in together. So she wouldn't have to go alone."

Tucker nodded. The guy was understanding. He *got* it.

"We'll all go in together," he said.

And we did. Tucker first, then me, and Savannah, squeaking slightly, bringing up the rear.

The prop room was about the size of a very small classroom, each wall covered from floor to ceiling with shelves on which were stashed props from old shows—everything from plastic flowers to fake turkeys to a full suit of armor. The people who'd already arrived were sitting in sort of a lopsided circle already.

My palms felt sweaty, and I pressed them to my skirt (why hadn't I changed out of my costume?) as I looked around to see who was there. Kelvin Black, fresh from his triumphant performance of "Sit Down, You're Rocking the Boat," was the first person I saw. He'd changed his clothes, and looked flushed and just slightly chunky in an Abercrombie T-shirt and jeans. Next to him was Andrew, the only other member of the Mission Choir except for me and Savannah. He looked a little impatient and distracted—as an eighth grader, he would have played before, so maybe things were taking a little too long for his liking. Fedora

Kravitz sat next to Andrew, with Ben Pfeiffer on her other side. Then Annabelle Peterson, who couldn't stop giggling and forming short twirls of her strawberry blond hair in her fingers. Next to her was Chris Seligman, who'd changed back into his head-to-toe black, and was chatting with Mia Kezdekian, who was on his other side. Mia was still wearing her Adelaide costume and the effect was somewhat . . . magnificent. Bud sat next to Mia, shouting something over several heads in Ben's direction. Predictably Delilah sat on Bud's other side, and I wondered if she planned on acting as his bodyguard. Because at this point, I couldn't imagine what Delilah was going to do when it was Bud's turn to spin. She did, now that I looked at her, have a fairly grim expression on her face. Scooter Nemo sat next to Delilah, wearing a white T-shirt with a hole over the shoulder, and a large trucker's cap that said "Got Milk?" on the brim. Delilah looked like she was trying to discreetly move away from Scooter, but I didn't know what difference that would make. They were still in a circle. If the bottle stopped, it stopped.

"Good, two more girls," said Annabelle. "We need one between Kelvin and Andrew, and one between Scooter and Kelvin."

Savannah and I exchanged a glance, and she went

and sat next to Andrew. I took the space on the other side of Kelvin.

"The circle looks too small," Annabelle continued. "Oh, now we have Tucker. And there's Dana."

Dana had come in just behind us, having been clearly undergoing some major primping. She was brushed and fluffed and made up within an inch of her life.

"How about Dana and I go right here," Tucker said, guiding Dana to the designated spot.

So it was Dana, not me, that ended up next to Tucker. Was that bad? Was that good? Was it less likely that the bottle would stop so close to home? Tucker was across the circle from me, not directly but off to one side. Was this helpful? Was it problematic? Delilah had made sure she sat next to Bud—was it best to sit next to the person you really liked? Had I already blown it? Stop overthinking!

Delilah stood up and raised her hand the way Mr. Romeo did, except no one stopped talking. I noticed she had a tiny Band-Aid right in the middle of her nose. Had it been there during the rehearsal? I had never been close enough to notice.

"Dudes, chillax!" yelled Ben Pfeiffer, and the noise slowly stopped.

"Okay. I want to welcome you all," Delilah said, "especially the little newbies, to our annual game of

Spin the Bottle, even though it's not opening night. The Bottle must spin on, right?"

She giggled a little, and her eyes bulged too far out of her head to look cute.

"So, there are a few ground rules I'd like to go over first."

"What are you, the self-appointed ref?" asked Mia, extending her long legs in front of her, and rearranging her hair behind her shoulders with one smooth, gorgeous shake of her head.

"Well, Mia," Delilah said, pronouncing Mia's name extremely slowly and with a lot of breathiness, as if she were addressing a very small, unintelligent child, "I am, as you know, president of the Drama Club, so it follows that—"

"And this, as we all know from our talk with Mr. Romeo today, is *not* an official Drama Club function. So you have no reason to put yourself up there bossing us around. Like our fearless leader said, it's not in your purrrrrrrrrrrr-view."

Delilah's hand fluttered to her chest and she glanced over at Bud, who was grinning at Mia. This seemed to enrage her.

"Don't spoil this for everyone else, Mia!" This time she spat Mia's name. "There are a few rules, and that's it. You're just delaying the game!"

She looked around the circle nodding, waiting

for other people to agree with her. No one said anything. Annabelle let out another giggle, but stifled it. Savannah and I exchanged startled looks. We hadn't expected things to start out so tensely. Then Fedora started to giggle, and the contagion spread. Soon all of the girls except Mia and Delilah were laughing, and even Savannah and I were smiling.

"You're trying to convince everybody that you're in charge, because what you really want is to make sure nobody kisses your boyfriend, since you ordered him not to play. And yet here he is," Mia said. "Anyway, why wouldn't it be okay for him to play since you are? Little bit of a double standard, huh Delilah?" Then she gave Delilah a wide and remarkably unpleasant smile.

Delilah stamped her foot.

"Keep it up, and you'll be disqualified!" she yelled.

Mia simply kept smiling.

"Delilah, you can't disqualify anybody, and there is nobody in charge of the game," said Tucker. "We had this argument last show, and the show before."

My heart beat its way out of my chest, all the way up my throat, and into my mouth, where it thunk-thunked violently.

"Let's just play," Tucker continued. "Same rules as always. When it's your turn, you spin the bottle clockwise. Whoever it points to, you kiss. If it's between two people, you spin again. If you're a girl and it points to a girl, or if it's boy/boy, you get a do-over."

Everybody was looking at Tucker, including me. He was so ridiculously handsome. His face was so kind, and his eyes so honest, and that lock of hair that brushed one eyebrow belonged in the Museum of Boy-tropolitan Art. The Spin the Bottle circle was my personal wheel of fortune. It could open the door to my future. Was it possible, if one of us had to kiss someone else, that we would ruin something that so far was perfect?

The bottle was already in the center of the room. It was a plastic 20-ounce bottle with a red label that said "RC Cola." I'd never heard of the brand, and wondered if it was a traditional bottle, produced from the shelves of the prop closet each year. As I stared at it, innocently lying motionless in the center of our circle, I started to feel sick. The bottle was so . . . there. So . . . real.

"President of the Club goes first, that's tradition," Delilah proclaimed. "Then we'll move clockwise to Scooter, and so on until we get to the end."

"You just want to make sure Bud goes last," Mia said, laughing. "You can't delay the inevitable, Lady D."

"No talking," commanded Delilah, which was obviously ridiculous and unlikely. But she was reaching for the bottle, and the group naturally hushed as she knelt down on both knees, took a deep breath, and gave the bottle a vigorous spin.

It was impossible to keep up with who the bottle was passing as it spun. My brain registered Ben, the OOMA (gasp), Bud, and Scooter, who was sitting right next to me. But the bottle had a lot of momentum, and it made a full circuit passing everyone two, maybe even three times before slowing. No one in the room seemed to be breathing. I certainly wasn't. My gaze was glued to the bottle as it wobbled slightly another eighth of a turn, then stopped.

It was pointing to Fedora. Everyone started laughing and talking at once.

"Delilah and Fedora sittin' in a tree . . ." shouted Ben.

"It's a do-over, everybody shut up!" Delilah said. She looked mad and relieved at the same time. I looked at Fedora's neighbors and theorized that Delilah had come very close to having to kiss either Andrew or Ben. I suspected neither of them were on the top of her list. Who would be on Delilah's wish list? Chris Seligman, maybe. Certainly the OOMA— even Delilah could not be blind to his magnificence. She could *use* him to make Bud jealous!

Before I realized what was happening, the bottle was on the move again. Round and round it went, and it took longer to stop this time. When it did, it pointed directly at Bud Gelcho. Delilah gave a triumphant squeal, and clapped her hands together.

"Pucker up, Bud—the ball and chain is coming!" yelled Scooter Nemo. Delilah gave him a nasty look, then walked back to Bud, who was doing his best to look bored and amused. Since Bud didn't stand, Delilah sat down next to him, which was where she'd been originally sitting anyway. She took his chin in her hand and turned his face toward her, and gave him a kiss on the lips. She tried to hold his chin in place and keep the kiss going, but the instant contact was made, Bud squirmed his face away. For the supposedly golden couple of the Drama Club, the smooch did not bode well for their future. Delilah kept up the appearance that all was well, snaking her arm around Bud's waist and producing a "happy" smile that even her own considerable acting ability could not make convincing.

Scooter was already up and reaching for the bottle. He gave it an enthusiastic spin, then chanted, "Go! Go! Go!" as it revolved. The bottle stopped when it was pointing to Fedora Kravitz. There was an immediate chorus of "Ooooooooooooooooooooooooo," except for Ben Pfeiffer, who looked a little miffed.

Scooter made a big show of smoothing his hair, tucking his shirt in, and doing some warm-up puckers with his lips. By the time he was taking a few deep knee bends, everyone was laughing hysterically, including Fedora. Scooter finished by cracking his knuckles, then he knelt next to Fedora, leaned in, and kissed her.

I hadn't felt weird about watching Bud and Delilah kiss, because they were sort of officially kissers anyway, and because the drama of the moment was irresistible. But it was strange to have Scooter and Fedora initiating a lip-lock and to simply sit there watching it, like it was on television.

For two people I'd never really seen interact before, it was a pretty enthusiastic kiss. It wasn't one of those over-lively kinds I've seen in movies, where the guy looks like he's lost something really important in the girl's mouth and he's going to root around until he finds it. This was a much simpler kiss, but it had an electricity to it that was kind of remarkable.

When the kiss was over and Scooter stood up, both his and Fedora's faces were bright red. They were also both grinning ear to ear. And Ben was scowling. It's hard to explain how I felt about it, except to say it was unexpected. Aside from flirting with myself in the bathroom mirror, all of my kissing practice had involved fruit, and it turns out I don't have much chemistry with anything in the citrus family. But the Scooter-Fedora kiss was like a communication of body and mind. More than ever, I wanted to kiss Tucker and feel those sparks from him. More than ever, I *didn't* want to kiss anyone else.

Now that Scooter was seated, all eyes were on me. So it could, theoretically, happen. Or it could, theoretically, not. I had spent so much time focusing on the perfection of kissing the OOMA. But I hadn't given much actual thought to the implications of kissing someone who was NOT the OOMA. Especially not after witnessing the real thing. And after finding out Tucker did like me.

"We don't have all day," Delilah said. "Move it."

I sat, paralyzed. I looked over at Tucker. He was looking right back at me. My stomach fluttered again.

"Let's go, newbie! SPIN!" Delilah barked.

I was frozen. Looking at Tucker. Being looked at by Tucker.

"Fine. I'll spin for you," Delilah said. And she bolted forward and gave the bottle a deft flick.

"Wait!" I cried, but the bottle had begun its spin of fate. In my mind I suddenly heard a game show audience shouting "Wheel! Of! Fortune!" My brain felt like it was spinning as fast as the bottle. I was shaking my head. I hadn't spun it myself. I didn't know what I wanted to do. Maybe if I shook my head hard enough it would fly off and roll across the room and I wouldn't have to kiss anyone.

The bottle passed Fedora.

Ben.

Annabelle.

It proceeded with excruciating slowness toward Tucker.

And passed him.

Wobbled in Dana's direction.

And came to a stop in front of Chris Seligman.

No.

My eyes were still locked with Tucker's. I knew at that instant that I would not be playing Spin the Bottle this night. Not because I didn't want to kiss a boy. But because there was only one boy in the world I *would* kiss.

"Don't just sit there," Delilah snapped. "It's Chris. Now get up."

I didn't.

"It doesn't count, Delilah," Tucker said. "She didn't spin the bottle—you did."

"Who cares who spun the stupid bottle?" Delilah cried. "It's landed on Chris, and she's gotta go and kiss him."

"No, I don't," I said. The sound of my voice surprised me, but the words were out. "It's totally not about you, Chris," I added quickly.

Chris shrugged. He didn't seem to care.

"I just realized . . . I can't kiss some random guy. It wouldn't be . . ." A vision of Harper suddenly flashed in my mind. "It wouldn't be authentic."

"What do you mean some *random* guy?" Delilah said shrilly. "That's the entire point!! You're just being a baby. You can't just come down here, then wimp out when it's your turn. If you're in the play, you *have* to play."

I stood up.

"No, I don't. There are plenty of things I *have* to do. But this isn't one of them." Harper had said this before, but this was the first time I'd realized that I really believed it too.

For the second time in one day, I truly didn't care what Delilah or the rest of them thought of me. I wasn't going to play. Nobody could change that.

Delilah flattened her lips into their meanest line.

"It's against the rules to leave once the game has started," she said.

"Shut up, Delilah," snapped Mia. "You need to beam back from fantasy land. *Nobody* is taking orders from you anymore. Not your boyfriend, and not the newbies. Give it up."

"Fine then," Delilah snapped. "This isn't a baby-sitting service. Go home to Mommy, Phoebe. Have some milk and cookies, and snuggle up with your Elmo doll."

It was such a stupid statement, it didn't need a response. I turned to leave, and Savannah suddenly jumped up.

"Actually, I'm going to take off too. See y'all at opening!"

Savannah shot me a nervous and happy smile and we walked to the door together. I didn't want to go without having some kind of conversation with Tucker, but we were making a big statement here and we had to go with it. Savannah went out first, and I followed. As I left, I heard Delilah speak up again.

"We shouldn't even let seventh graders *be* in Drama Club," Delilah was saying. "I'm going to suggest to Mr. Romeo—"

"Will someone just shut that girl up!" Mia shouted.

I took that opportunity to pull the door closed.

Savannah was standing in the hallway, eyes wide.

"You have no idea how relieved I am that you did that. You are so brave! I mean, it sounded so cool and everything, playing Spin the Bottle. But when it started for real, I just knew I wasn't ready for it. And I didn't think there was any way I'd be brave enough to walk out, and suddenly you got up and said you weren't playing. Phee . . . you are my hero!"

"Aw, shucks," I said, grinning.

"Seriously," Savannah stated. "You are. How did you work up the courage to stand up to Delilah? Did you feel you just weren't ready to play too?"

I took a deep breath.

"It's weird. For a long time I really did want to play. But there's this one guy that I really . . . like. And every time I thought about the game, all I could imagine was the bottle pointing to *him*. And tonight I kind of realized that he sort of likes me too. How could I know that, and then kiss just anyone?"

Savannah let out a little sigh.

"That's so romantic," she said. Then to my surprise, she added, "You are a girl with integrity."

It was so like something Harper would say, I was taken aback. There was definitely a lot more to the Blond Cherubic Newbie than I had thought.

"I'm going to call my mom to come pick me up-I've got my cell in my bag. Do you want a ride?"

"I'd love one," I said with relief.

"Great. I'm going to run to the bathroom first. Can you hang out a sec?"

"Sure," I said. Actually disappearing into the bathroom along with Savannah was very tempting, so I wouldn't have to stand all alone in the hallway looking stupid. But I told myself I didn't have to care about that stuff anymore. And boy, did that ever turn out to be an excellent choice.

Because while I was standing there waiting, the door to the prop room opened, and Tucker came out.

"Awesome. I hoped you'd waited," he said. "There were a few things I wanted to say to Delilah before I took off. Things most of us should have told her a long time ago. Are you okay?"

Was I okay. Was. I. Okay. About as okay as if I had just won my first Oscar.

"I'm okay," I said. I had this stupid grin on my face. Tucker was starting to get one too, only his had that dimple.

"Delilah was way out of line, she's gone all commando this year. Good for you for standing up to her."

"It was easy," I heard myself saying. "Because I didn't want to . . . Because I only wanted to . . . "

Tucker took a step toward me. My knees shook.

"Me neither," he said. "Me too."

And then. He reached over. And kissed. My. Lips.

It was soft, and brief, and there were more sparks flying than over the Statue of Liberty on the Fourth of July. Then it was over. He smiled. And as if the moment had been written for the stage, Savannah made her entrance from the bathroom.

"Hey guys!"

"Yahoka," I whispered, nodding and trying to smile and not cry with happiness.

"Catch you tomorrow?" Tucker whispered.

"Catch me tomorrow," I replied.

He gave Savannah a little wave, and turned and trotted quickly up the stairs.

"Hey—so my mom will be here in—" Savannah stopped suddenly, examining my face. "Are you all right?"

I grinned.

"I am, Savannah. I am ALL RIGHT."

And I was just that. So I was a little flawed. Tucker was too. But everyone had their flaws, and I knew that in spite of mine, I *was* remarkable. Harper had always thought so. And now Mr. Romeo did too.

And so, most remarkably, did the Object of My Affection.

CHAPTER FIFTEEN
Curtain Call

Opening night. How often did a girl get a night like this? I imagined how, tomorrow morning, I would share a bowl of steamed rice for breakfast with Harper after our opening night sleep-over, while we went over every single moment of both this night and last night from her perspective, and from mine. Particularly the bits that involved Tucker and the Non-Spin-the-Bottle-Kiss. But for now, it was all still happening. The best night of my life was unfolding all around me, and I wanted to dig my heels in and hold on to it so it would never fade into the past.

When I got to the girls' dressing room, there was a rose laid out on the counter next to the hook where my costume hung. There was a tiny card with my name on it. On the back was written: "Break a leg. Tucker."

The traditional theatrical sentiment of good wishes has always been "Break a leg." And I'd always dreamed of someone saying it to me on my first opening night. I just never imagined it would be. Him.

So I had quite a long list of things to be simultaneously thrilled and queasy about. And I had a lot of company. The whole cast was giddy with excitement. With one exception.

Delilah was definitely not acting like her usual self. She was glum and silent. People steered clear of her. It was so strange, such a departure from the way things had always been, that I felt bad for her. As Mr. Romeo was calling places, Delilah just sat at her dressing table, in full costume and makeup, staring at the floor.

I was almost out the door, when I hesitated.

"Hey. Delilah," I said.

She looked up at me, and scowled slightly.

"Break a leg!"

She didn't say anything. But she did get up and brush past me. Whatever had happened or was happening, Delilah still had a bit of the regal air left in her.

Standing in places onstage, behind the lowered

curtain, I was almost hopping with anticipation for the show to start. I also wanted to hold on to this moment, standing here with my fellow actors, hearing the buzz and hum of the crowd in the seats, listening to the little orchestra making their final instrument tunings. Trying to remember exactly which seats my parents were in so I could sneak peeks at them. I was happier than I'd ever imagined I could be. And I wanted to stop time and savor this moment forever.

But the curtain was rising, and the lights were shining on us, and the musicians were playing the opening bars of "Follow the Fold."

The show was on.

Noel Coward, the great playwright/composer/director/actor, once sang, "I couldn't have liked it more, oh no, I couldn't have liked it more." How true. When I wasn't onstage, I planted myself in the wings and watched every precious moment. Everyone rocked. When Chris Seligman had his scenes, you couldn't take your eyes off him. Ben Pfeiffer had the audience rolling in the aisles with his thick gangster accent and his tough dumb-guy swagger. Mia practically stole the show vamping as Adelaide. And in spite of her pre-show depression, Delilah pulled out all the stops as Sarah. She had to pause a few times after her songs because the audience kept breaking out into spontaneous applause. Whatever depths she had sunk to, they didn't affect her onstage. I'll be the first to admit it. Delilah Fortescue was still a great actress.

I stood in the wings, watching Delilah and Bud doing one of their big numbers, a song called "I've Never Been in Love Before." Delilah's voice was sweet and clear. Not at all what you'd expect if you . . . well. If you knew her.

"Did you hear she almost didn't go on?" a voice whispered in my ear.

Savannah was standing so close behind me, I was almost giving her a piggyback.

"You mean Delilah?" I whispered back.

Savannah nodded.

"You know how she had that little Band-Aid on her nose? Apparently after final notes this afternoon Mia reached over and ripped it right off her face."

Since exclaiming loudly was impossible, I shot my eyebrows up and opened my mouth as wide as it would go. Savannah nodded vigorously.

"And supposedly Delilah starts yelling 'I'm not contagious! I'm not contagious!'" Savannah whispered.

"Wait. Contagious as in the chicken pox?"

Savannah nodded, looking scandalized.

"She was hiding it, not just so she could go on tonight, but so she could play Spin the Bottle yesterday! Since Bud was definitely playing, I guess Delilah was dead set on being there too."

"But she might have infected half the cast!"

"I know, right?" Savannah whispered.

There was the sound of thunderous applause from the audience. Delilah and Bud had finished their number, which meant it was intermission. I dragged Savannah toward the staircase that led to the prop room, so we wouldn't run into Bud and Delilah as they came offstage.

"Okay, I'm totally confused now," I said, relieved to be able to continue this conversation without whispering.

"There's more," Savannah said. "Mr. Romeo was right there during the whole thing. Which I'm sure was part of Mia's plan. So apparently he called the school nurse and had her come over. And the nurse examined this thing on Delilah's nose, while she kept saying nobody needed to worry because she wasn't going to give anyone the chicken pox because she wasn't contagious."

"But how would she know that? How can you have chicken pox and *not* be contagious?"

"You can't," Savannah replied. "She was more like, insisting it was true because she wanted it to be.

So then the nurse finishes looking at this thing Delilah has on her nose and she—the nurse—turns to Mr. Romeo and says, 'The young lady is right—she is *not* contagious.' And Mr. Romeo asks what she means, and the nurse says, 'The young lady does not have the chicken pox. She has a rather remarkably tenacious pimple. Unpleasant, but not contagious.' Mia Kezdekian heard the whole thing and told Andrew, who told me. That's exactly what she said—unpleasant . . . but not contagious."

"But Delilah didn't know it was just a zit?" I said, outrage rising in my stomach. "She really thought she had the chicken pox, and she tried to hide it under a Band-Aid!"

"Yep. And now she's saying she knew all along, and she was just kidding about the chicken pox," Savannah explained.

That was low. Really, really low. I wouldn't have thought even Delilah could do something so insensitive. Being in control, calling the shots, and being the lead was all she cared about, even if it meant infecting her castmates with chicken pox, and possibly bringing the entire production to a halt. All for something that would be over in just a few days.

It was almost impossible to believe that I'd once idolized this girl, and thought her friendship was my ticket to acceptance. Instead, I'd openly defied Delilah in front of the entire club, and they all seemed to still like me just fine. Even though it had only been a few weeks, it seemed that years had passed since the day Delilah had come to my house, and I had thought it so flattering and significant.

Intermission was only ten minutes, and the Hot Box Girls were already getting in place for their hysterically funny bit called "Take Back Your Mink." The show was halfway over. We were just a few songs away from the Mission Choir's last big number, singing backup for "Sit Down, You're Rocking the Boat." I wanted to make sure and remind Dana not to stand up during the wrong verse tonight. My parents were in the audience, after all. And so were Dr. and Mrs. Tanaka.

The more I tried to hang on to every moment, the faster time passed. Savannah, Andrew, Dana, and I stood offstage waiting for our cue to walk onstage and into the mission for Sergeant Sarah's big Save-a-Sinner meeting. We'd be mostly onstage for the rest of the show.

And I had to say, through our rollicking backup singing (with no flub by Dana this time), through Adelaide and Nathan Detroit's final song, to the reprise of the Hot Box Girls just before the double wedding, everything went perfectly. I let myself relish my very last line, in spite of the fact that it was spoken along with the other members of the Mission Choir, because it was my last first opening night ever. There'd be many more opening nights, but never another first one.

As the lights blazed up to full on Adelaide and Nathan and Sarah and Sky standing center stage, Savannah, Andrew, Dana, and I took off our Salvation Army hats and saluted the four as we shouted, "To the happy couples!" Then Savannah sang the first line of "For She's a Jolly Good Fellow" to Delilah, our Sergeant Sarah. And when I heard her sing the line clearly and loudly in her sweet, choir-girl voice, I felt a rush of pride for Savannah. Then the Mission Choir picked up the next few lines, and finally the whole cast joined in, and we segued into the "Guys and Dolls" reprise.

If you've never stood on a stage with a big group of people and sung something, you should really give it a try. I can honestly say there is no feeling like it in the world. The lights are blinding, your heart is pounding, you can feel the audience even if you can't really see them, and all those voices singing creates this incredible energy you could cut with a knife. And while we stood there in that moment, the whole cast singing the final number on opening night, I felt like I really belonged. I was one of them. And they were my friends too, most of them.

I even felt a tiny sliver of affection for Delilah. She was more deeply flawed than most of us. But she was also remarkable too, as an actress. No matter what else had happened or who she turned out to really be, I still respected her for that.

When the last line was delivered and the music was over, the entire cast lined up onstage for a curtain call. I was exactly where and what I'd always wanted to be. No more Inner and Outer. Just Me. And I wouldn't have changed a thing about that moment or myself, not for the world.

I was standing close to the wings, and as our audience clapped and hooted and rose to their feet, the curtain came down and I dashed offstage for a moment, past the place where I'd once barfed, because I'd caught sight of my favorite person in the world. Harper Tanaka.

"Aren't you supposed to be in the booth?" I cried.

"Not after the last cue," she said. "I wanted to give you a hug, I wanted to be in this with you while it's still happening."

"You *are* in this with me!" I cried. "We have to go out for second bow—they're bringing the curtain up again. Come on!"

"No!"

Harper leaned hard in the other direction like her

basset hound did when she tried to take him for a walk. But I'd learned many things about the Chipmunk Death Grip from Savannah, and I hung on tight and dragged my best friend along, and the next thing you knew we were both onstage, standing next to Savannah, who immediately moved over to make room for us.

I could see Harper's parents laughing and pointing in surprise to see their daughter onstage. My parents were waving frenetically, and my mother was dabbing at her eye with a tissue.

The cast was shouting and gesturing, and Mr. Romeo appeared—he actually seemed to glide up onto the stage. He looked pristine and magnificent in a jet-black suit with creases so sharp, they might cut something, completely unflustered as he took his own well-deserved bow, then slipped away backstage.

I beamed at my fellow castmates as they took bow after bow. Tucker saluted me, and I saluted back. Ben Pfeiffer had started a kind of chorus line kick, which Romalla Lee Um and Fedora Kravitz were imitating. Chris Seligman had his hands clasped in front of him and his eyes closed as he periodically made little bows. Mia and Bud were doing some kind of tango, and Delilah stood to one side, a frozen smile on her mouth that was not quite up to her usual theatrical standards. So much work, so much drama, all for this moment. Was it worth it? Totally.

On Sunday afternoon we would perform our final matinee, then the sets would come down and the costumes would go back into the shop and all traces of our work would be gone. Soon auditions for the spring production would be announced. Maybe Delilah and Bud would keep their perfect record and grab the starring couple role. From what I had seen, it was more likely that by then they'd no longer be a couple. Perhaps Mia Kezdekian would eclipse them with her own enormous talent. And who knows? Maybe I'd land a juicy part myself. Mr. Romeo himself, after all, expected great things from me.

And what about the next game of Spin the Bottle? Only time would tell where I would be then. Right now the only bottle I was interested in was one that was filled with twelve ounces of ice cold Coca-Cola. For the moment, Spin the Bottle had nothing to offer me. I was here, onstage, after all. Harper was still my best friend. And the Object of My Affection had given me a kiss and a rose.

I was flawed. I was remarkable. I was me.